Nikolaĭ M. Przhevalskiĭ, Edward D. Morgan

From Kulja

across the Tian Shan to Lob-Nor

Nikolaï M. Przhevalskiï, Edward D. Morgan

From Kulja
across the Tian Shan to Lob-Nor

ISBN/EAN: 9783337256173

Printed in Europe, USA, Canada, Australia, Japan

Cover: Foto ©Andreas Hilbeck / pixelio.de

More available books at **www.hansebooks.com**

THE

WREATHED CROSS

AND

OTHER POEMS,

AESTHETIC AND RELIGIOUS.

BY

REV. D. Y. HEISLER, A. M.,

AUTHOR OF "THE FATHERS OF THE GERMAN REFORMED CHURCH IN
EUROPE AND AMERICA," AND "LIFE-PICTURES OF THE PRODIGAL
SON, A GIFT-BOOK FOR THE MILLION."

"Gather up the Fragments."

EASTON, PA.
FREE PRESS STEAM PUBLISHING HOUSE.
1879.

EL

TO MY

ESTEEMED FRIEND AND PRECEPTOR,

PROF. WILLIAM M. NEVIN, Esq.,

THIS

Little Volume

IS

GRATEFULLY INSCRIBED.

PREFACE.

THIS unpretending little volume is made up of Poems written during my leisure hours, and, with slight exceptions, in the exact order in which they are now published. Quite a number of them were composed on special occasions, and by request; some of them for children and young persons, which, accordingly, are gotten up in a style and language adapted to the taste and capacities of the parties for whom they were designed. This fact will account for the peculiar style and versification of some of the pieces. They are the simple echoes of the heart, and now come before the public without any pretensions—claiming no special merit, either literary or poetic. All they seek, is, to be useful and entertaining to persons of a chaste and earnest spirit, by presenting important popular and religious truths in language, simple, direct, and pleasing—aided by rythm and numbers.

For reasons which are deemed satisfactory, a few very early productions have been retained; for which we beg the reader's indulgence. It is hard to disown a child, however uncomely it may be. The book, indeed, does not profess to be a selection of choice Poems, only, but rather an artless collection of fugitive pieces, given very much in the form and order in which they were composed. We ask that this fact may be kept in mind while forming a judgment on their merits. The word AESTHETIC, found on the Title-page, is employed to designate those pieces, which, though not strictly religious, do yet treat of the true and beautiful in Nature and Providence, and, therefore, ought not to be stigmatized as profane, or secular, even, in the popular sense of these terms.   They come legitimately within the sphere of the human, the ethical, the aesthetic, being, in their nature and tendency, pure, chaste, elevating, and refining !

Whilst the language and style, as well as the subjects of the several compositions, are, thus, simple and unpretending, it is nevertheless hoped that they will not be found wanting in that refinement and delicacy of feeling and sentiment, and that chasteness of thought and expression, which are classed among the chief elements of true poetry.

The publication of these Poems, it may be added, is owing to the partiality and expressed wishes of a few personal friends, fully as much as to the Author's own judgment of propriety and duty in the case.   His only wish, now, is—that, in their present form, they may serve to amuse and gratify these special and interested friends, and, at the same time, afford true comfort and spiritual edification to his fellow pilgrims, generally, on Life's weary way— to the praise and glory of Him "from whom cometh down every good and perfect gift."

EASTON, PA., Easter Monday, 1879.

CONTENTS.

viii CONTENTS.

X CONTENTS.

PROEM—EXCELSIOR.

The mind plays queen—her Empire wide and firm,
Her Coronet of sparkling gems and gold—
Her Sceptre mighty, and her sway supreme ;
Endowed with rarest gifts—with potencies
On the realms supernal well-nigh trenching.
Yet, crude and primitive, the mind is weak,
Shackled, and in its progress stayed—inapt,
"And of its dole restrict."—Immured within
Its prison-house of clay, and captive held,
Impatient tho' it yearns and frets—it can't
Exert at once, its own sweet native force ;
Its range, conditioned, widens by degrees.
At times, indeed, it mounts with eagle-wing
The whirlwinds dizzy chariot, and, enshrined
In royal state, brings forth, in splendid forms,
The lofty thoughts imagination moulds !
At times, again, descending deep to scenes
Of philosophic strife, it fain would pluck
From off the sacred shrine the golden fruit.
But flights, like these, and dives to regions deep,
Where Nature's scenes, sublime, enchant the soul,
Belong, alas, to minds mature and cultured,
Skilled in lofty science—enriched with stores
Of ancient and of modern lore, high-prized.
The progress, which, in mounting step by step
The giddy heights of truth and knowledge deep,

The mind achieves, these pages fain would show.
At diff'rent points of life, my pen shall draw
Some pictures to mark the mental vigor—
Some lines by which, hereafter, I may trace
The progress of the mind; and, while I thus
Record its silent growth, may all conspire
To fill, with sentiments of grateful love,
My soul, elate for God's rich bounty shared,
And crown with honors high my blessed Lord!

The Wreathed Cross.

O Lamb of God—the pure—
  I long for Thee alone,
Thy blood doth peace secure,
  Thy wounds for sin atone ;
And, counting all things loss,
  I fix my hopes above,
And twine around Thy cross
  A wreath of purest love !

When sadness o'er me creeps,
  And gloomy shades prevail,
When night its vigil keeps,
  And passions fierce assail—
Then, Dearest Jesus, be
  My soul's sweet morning star ;
Thy light shall comfort me,
  Bright gleaming from afar !

Around the hallowed cross
  The heart's affections twine,
And, midst the heaviest loss,
  Their gushing streams combine;
They form a mighty flood,
  With genial warmth aglow,
And find, in Jesus' blood,
  A sweet and placid flow!

O wondrous cross—to me
  The source of purest joy—
From condemnation free,
  Sweet tho'ts my heart employ.
I upward look to Thee,
  O Lamb of God, most dear,
And, in Life's book, I see
  My pardon full and clear!

When light within doth shine,
  And sheds sweet comfort round,
When every blessing's mine,
  And joys supreme abound—
'Tis, then, I think of Thee,
  Dear Jesus, and Thy cross,
And, O, this comforts me,
  My gain stands in Thy loss!

When days grow dark and drear,
  And nights are thick with gloom,
When friends nor pleasures cheer,
  Nor peace in me finds room,
O, then, I turn mine eyes
  To dear Golgotha's brow,
And every shadow flies—
  Sweet peace is round me now!

Thy bleeding love, dear Lord,
　My trembling soul assures,
The promise of Thy word
　My future bliss secures ;
For, in Thy wondrous cross,
　With sacred blood bedewed,
I hail, 'midst outward loss,
　My inner life renewed !

What honors shall I bring,
　Dear Saviour, to Thy name ?
What anthems shall I sing
　To Thee of ancient fame ?
My heart, aglow with love,
　To highest praise aspires,
And, from the realms above,
　Thy life my spirit fires !

O wondrous gift to me,
　This gift of life divine,
Conjoined my soul with Thee,
　Make Thou me wholly Thine ;
My life I bring to Thee,
　Nor aught esteem I loss,
For what is dear to me,
　I twine around Thy cross !

And, if, with cares opprest,
　I wander here and there,
And find no soothing rest,
　No answer to my pray'r,
Then, hail I Jesus, slain,
　Fixed on the crimson cross ;
And gladly count that gain
　Which was my greatest loss !

My heart, now calm and free,
  Is filled with love divine,
And, gazing still on Thee,
  I hail Thee, Jesus, mine;
Then round the cross is seen
  A halo bright and fair,
And earth and sky, I ween,
  Are bathed in fulgent air!

How sweet is life, and bright,
  When Thy free grace is nigh;
How soft and clear the light,
  Which cometh from on high;
And yet, my dearest Lord,
  I need Thee every hour,
I need Thy conq'ring word,
  I need Thy saving power!

When Death, with sable wing,
  Sweeps o'er my pilgrim way;
When foes to conflict bring
  Their hosts in fierce array—
Then, Christ, in Thee secure,
  I'll hasten to Thy cross—
Thy blood doth make me pure,
  Thy grace repairs my loss!

At length, when life is o'er,
  And all its tears are shed,
When placed on Canaan's shore,
  Amid the sainted dead—
Then, Jesus, free from dross,
  I'll worship Thee above,
And twine around Thy cross
  A wreath of PERFECT love!

MEDITATIONS—A SOLILOQUY.

Infinite Goodness! say, what meed of praise,
What love, what gratitude is due Thy grace?
What sentiments should in my bosom glow,
And from my pen what tho'ts exclusive flow?

When all Thy varied mercies I review—
Thy kindness shown, each morn and evening new,
Each want supplied from out Thy boundless stores,
My heart o'erflows, my wondering soul adores!

And shall I hush?—conceal these gifts divine,
And in this swelling heart my tho'ts confine?
Or shall I speak Thy love—Thy grace declare,
And with me cause each, ALL, these gifts to share?

Great source of Light—do Thou my bosom fill
With tho'ts that live and gently sway the will;
And may my soul—illumined from above,
Incessant feel and gladly speak Thy love!

Where'er I stray or turn my ravished eyes,
Such scenes of grandeur to my vision rise—
Such beauty, grace, and loveliness combine,
As show the hand that made them is divine!

Here on this earth and in yon vaulted sky,
A thousand tokens of Thy Love I 'spy,—
Each twinkling star appears a gem of light,
To beautify the varied scenes of night.

And, O, when I with steady gaze survey
The radiant scenes of night and charms of day,
My spirit, winged with rays of purest love,
In vision soars to sweetest joys above!

Yet other wonders, more stupendous still,
Do the blest pages of Thy volume fill—
'Tis there, I ween, the depths of love divine
Do in their most resplendent beauties shine!

'Tis there we learn—the only wisdom this—
The way to present joy and future bliss;
How sinners lost may be restored to God
And saved by virtue of redeeming blood!

How condescending and how strangely kind
Seems the Divine Restorer of mankind;
His love so boundless, so exceeding great,
He died—to glory changed our vile estate!

'Twas not for self the Son of God came down,
And cheerful wore on earth the Martyr's crown;
His loving Heart, by pure compassion moved,
Urged him to leave what He so dearly loved.

He left his Home on high, and HERE became
A man of deepest sorrow, grief and shame;
Betrayed by secret foes—by friends denied,
To court and judgment led—then crucified!

My dearest Lord—my Saviour and my God,
What varied paths of anguish hast Thou trod,
And yet how feebly burns the flame of love,
O take my Heart—fix all my thoughts above!

'Mid trials sore and persecution's frown,
Help me to wear, with THEE, the thorny crown;
And when Life's every ill I've meekly borne,
Then take me, Lord, where mourners cease to mourn.

THE DATE PALM.

Majestic—in the barren waste—
The Date Palm springeth up in haste;
Straight, as an arrow shot from bow,
Doth it, the prince of fruit trees grow,
In verdure fair, 'mid burning sands,
The pride and boast of desert stands;
As upward to the clouds it shoots,
It, also, deeply strikes its roots.
'Tis needful that its base be firm
To guarranty a lengthened term;
For, when the tree so lofty grows,
The tempest, also, rudely blows;
And, then, the tree, so slim and straight,
Disports a top of extra weight—
The trunk encircling far aloft,
Are leaves, amazing, thick and soft;
And then the fruit, in clusters found,
Grows thick and close the tree around,
Which, as it may be well supposed,
Is oft to passing winds exposed;
These, sweeping o'er the arid plain,
And, all things striking in their train,
Would hurl the giant to the grouud,
Were not its moorings solid found.
But, most of all, the tree, designed
For wand'ring hordes to wilds assigned,

Is thus conserved and useful made,
With food uniting grateful shade;
And, groaning 'neath its precious boon,
It, shelt'ring, cheers the heart at noon;
And eve and morn the Bedouin
For food and shelter there is seen.
These children of the desert wild,
By its sweet umbrage thus beguiled,
And, feasting on its luscious fruit,
Make it the object of pursuit—
Accounting it the richest boon,
A grateful screen from sun and moon;
For, pleasant tho' its fruit may be,
Its cooling shade, as each can see,
Is equally as dear to them—
The wand'ring, restless sons of Shem.
But, Oh! the wonders of this tree,
Are greater yet by far, you see,
For every part is useful found,
From top e'en down unto the ground:
The trunk elastic wood doth yield,
To furnish them with bow and shield;
The bark is twisted into cords,
To string the bows of savage lords;
The leaves, to roof the tents, are spread,
Or, beaten soft, they form their bed;
The fruit yields them a grateful drink
Which helps the Arab mind to think;
Nor prize they wine and date alone,
A usance greater far they own;
The seeds, esteemed of equal good,
Do form the patient camel's food.
But who may venture, thus, to state
The endless uses of the Date?
It comfort brings to man and beast,

And in the desert spreads a feast.
Its wondrous uses, Arabs say,
Are—one to each recurring day ;
Three hundred, thus, and sixty-five,
Which keep them all the year alive.
No marvel, then, that they should call
The Palm—the noblest tree. of all,
Esteem it God's best gift to them,
The wild and roving sons of Shem ;
And for it yield, with hearts elate,
Their thanks each day to ALLAH¸great !

REFLECTIONS.

Majestic Tree !—In deserts wild,
Men laud thee for thy gifts so mild ;
Nor would to thee our hearts deny
This tribute of laudations high ;
For great thy patent virtues are,
And hidden ones surpass them far,
If not in number, yet in grade—
Of nobler things the emblems made.
The trunk, so lofty and so straight,
Doth show the Christian's high estate ;
Thy leaves and branches, up so far,
The signet of his virtues are ;
Thy luscious fruit, so rich and sweet,
Yields of his life an emblem meet ;
Thy branches, in their fadeless green,
Are oft in glad processions seen ;
Thus, when the Lord, His labors closed,
To enter Salem's gates proposed,
His princely honor to maintain,
Thy branches graced the royal train ;
For multitudes, on that bright day,
With palm and vestments strewed the way !
Yet further, still, thy fame extends

To higher worlds and nobler ends;
For, when His glories were displayed,
By Saints, in snow-white robes arrayed,
Then of that bright, triumphant band
Each one a palm-branch bore in hand ;
The Palm—a sign of vict'ry gained,
The glist'ning robes of bliss obtained!
Their robes made white in Jesus' blood,
Their vict'ry speaks the purple flood ;
And cross and crown, in sweet accord,
Bear witness to our blessed Lord,
While robes of white and branches green,
As emblems of His work, are seen :
The Palm is, thus, in honor found—
In em'rald wreaths the cross around!

CHILDHOOD.

When Fancy sweeps the distant past,
    And wakes to life what happened then,
The fairy things appear so fast
    That they defy the readiest pen ;
Each moment brings some magic form
    With rain-bow tints all fair and bright;
The day knows naught of cloud or storm,
    And moon and stars illume the night!

How radiant shines the rising sun—
    How soft and fair the landscape round!
How sweet the hours, and full of fun,
    And woods and hills with song resound!
Sweet days of Childhood! O how dear
    That age so free from sin and care!
How brilliant all things then appear,
    How well the little pilgrims fare!

Their joys, at early morn begun,
 Are glowing yet at day's decline;
And e'en the gleams of setting sun
 Still in their hearts effulgent shine.
How HAPPY, thus, at dawn of day,
 When Nature seems so bright and fair,
How spry and blithesome in their play,
 With hearts as free and light as air!

Out in the fields and meadows, they
 With agile limbs and spirits high,
Pursue the gold-wing'd bugs of May,
 Or chase the painted butterfly;
Sweet roses, found in hedge or field,
 With eager haste they gather there,
And bogs and fens must likewise yield
 Their share of lilies pure and fair!

Thus, roaming gay, o'er hill and dale,
 They make the boundless forest ring,
With sportive shouts their hearts regale,
 And, laughing, their sweet ditties sing.
The trees must cater to their wants,
 The festooned vines afford a swing,
And bush and bough, in gloomy haunts,
 Must each its share of pleasure bring.

Sweet age of innocence and joy—
 Of festive days and dreamless nights,
What sorrow can thy peace destroy,
 What grief alloy thy pure delights!
How, often, from Life's scenes of care,
 My longing heart reverts to thee,
Once more thy peerless joys to share,
 While mingling in thy childish glee!

O could we but this scene prolong,
    And still possess, without alloy,
The gladsome hours, the thrill, the song,
    The echo of that earlier joy!
Ah! could we but in fancy bring
    Those fragrant seasons back again,
How would we then rejóice and sing,
    And, rapt, forget each tort'ring pain!

Blest time of innocence and love,
    So like that primal age of earth,
When, in each fragrant field and grove,
    Was heard the voice of sacred mirth;
When ev'ry tree, and shrub, and flower,
    In ceaseless flow, sweet incense breathed,
And in, and through fair Eden's bow'r,
    Each object was in beauty wreathed!

That season ne'er shall come again,
    To bring its sweet enjoyments back;
My time is that of grief and pain,
    In comforts tho' it doth not lack;
But, looking o'er the beauteous past,
    In fancy, free from sin and pain,
I hope, thro' grace divine, at last
    To be a child in truth again!

ASLEEP IN JESUS.

There is a calm, a sweet repose
    For those who sleep in Jesus blest;
They safely 'hide, secure from foes,
    And on the Saviour's bosom rest.

THE NATIVITY.

The shepherds, 'neath an Eastern sky,
    Were watching o'er their flocks by night,
When, suddenly, there gleamed on high
    A splendor 'bove the noon-day light;
For, lo, an Angel from the throne
    In glory came upon them there;
A heavenly light around them shone,
    And they, afraid, the glory share!

Then kindly did the Angel say—
    "Fear not, glad tidings you I bring;
For unto you is born to-day
    In Bethlehem a Saviour—king,
Great joy and gladness now shall see
    All kindred tribes of human kind;
And of this joy—the sign shall be
    In manger that the babe ye find."

The story scarcely had been told,
    Then brilliant forms swept o'er the plain;
A multitude their Prince enfold,
    Loud praising God in lofty strain,
Exultant shouting—as they sang—
    "Be glory now to God most High,"
"And peace on earth," the chorus rang,
    "Good will to men," both far and nigh!

Soon as the charming song had ceased,
   And angel-bands to heav'n were gone,
The shepherds, from their spell released,
   Were, thoughtful, left to muse alone;
And each, instinctive, said and thought,
   "Come now—let's go to Bethlehem,
There see the wonder God hath wrought,
   The wonder God hath wrought for men !"

Still prompted by th' angelic song,
   The shepherds haste to reach the spot,
And, by the spirit borne along,
   Their feet, so nimble, weary not;
Anon they reach the destined place,
   Their joy—what mortal can define?
The Angel's word, fulfilled, they trace,
   With Mary find the babe Divine !

O wondrous sight! O bliss divine !
   With sacred joy their hearts o'erflow,
Th' incarnate myst'ry they opine,
   And worship Jesus—bending low;
Then hast'ning to their tented fields,
   They all along the news proclaim;
Enraptured, glad, each bosom yields
   A grateful song to Jesus' Name!

REST FOR THE WEARY.

There is for weary pilgrims found
   A rest from all their toils and cares,
A Home, where joys supreme abound,
   A bliss, wherein each wand'rer shares;
To this dear rest—this home above,
Are gathered all the sons of love !

NEW-YEAR'S VISION.

Once struggling up a rugged steep,
  What TIME I cannot say,
I reached the mountain's lofty peak,
  Thence sloping either way—
And down the hill on either side
  I saw a spacious plain,
It seemed much like a chequer-board,
  Tho' not alike the TWAIN:

The ONE, o'erhung by gloomy shades,
  Without ONE brilliant ray,
The only Light by mortals seen,
  Was like to "dawn of day;"
The other, 'neath a cloudless sky,
  Was brighter far, and fair,
And yet the plain seemed varied by
  A shadow here and there!

Across this chequered plain I 'spied
  The pathway trod by me;
The length—if I remember right—
  Was thirty miles and three;
Enough—my sluggish spirit seemed
  Aroused to strong desire,
And in my waking eyes now beamed
  The meditative fire.

While gazing pensive on the scenes,
   Which 'round this pathway lay,
And anxiously concerned to know
   How I had passed that way;
An Angel, clothed in purest white,
   Stood by—with wisdom rife—
And kindly offered to unfold
   The myst'ry of my life!

He gently raised his hand and said
   "Far yonder—do you see
A spot in richest garb arrayed,
   From sorrows mostly free,
And, in that spot of innocence,
   An object strange and new,
An INFANT watched by Providence,
   That infant once were you!

"The garden gate is open wide,
   The infant, now a boy,
Is out among the pit-falls seen,
   Of laughter full and joy—
E'en there God's arm protected him,
   But HOW no mortal knew,
Unharmed the wayward boy is seen,
   That wayward boy—were you!

"Full out upon Life's chequered plain,
   More perilous than all,
Behold what crowds of heedless youth
   Are yearly seen to fall;
But ONE, by sovereign grace, is seen
   In Christ created new;
That rescued one—O favored youth—
   That RESCUED one—were you!

"And now upon this lofty ridge,
  Of manhood's riper years,
Review Life's imperfections all,
  With penitential tears—
And, O, with manly gratitude
  In every such review,
Confess the Grace of Him who could
  Such mercy grant to YOU!"

Thus far the Angel : When he ceased
  My heart grew faint within ;
I saw me, with a vasty crowd,
  Still here exposed to sin—
While down on yonder side the ridge,
  Dark lay the gloomy plain ;
I begged him to my friends and me
  The FUTURE to explain.

In answer to my earnest pray'r,
  The Angel friend replied ;
"To mortals what is future yet,
  Is wisely here denied—
Be quiet, then, and childlike look
  To Him alone who knows ;
Whatever lies within this plain
  The Future will disclose !

"One thing or two I fain would tell,
  And solemn things they are,
How sinners may escape from hell,
  And life eternal share ;
One Light—the light of life—is come
  To chase the gloom away,
And thro' the darkest shades of night
  To lead to endless day.

" God, in the gospel of His Son,
    Invites His children home,
And offers 'grace' to cheer them on,
    Each FOE to overcome ;
Gives Faith to conquer death and hell,
    And Hope to make them strong,
And Love, the bond of perfectness,
    To bind the happy throng.

And see what boundless stores of grace
    In Jesus Christ are found,
Life, peace, and joy to every soul,
    That hears the blissful sound ;
And in His WORD the choicest rules
    To mortal man are given—
Directions how to walk secure
    Thro' yonder plain to Heaven !"

'Tis well—I knew it must be so
    Just as the Angel said ;
'Tis rashness to attempt to know
    That which is future yet ;
O God ! may I be satisfied
    With what each good man hath,
Thy WORD—"A LAMP TO GUIDE MY FEET,
    A LIGHT UNTO MY PATH."

THE EPIPHANY.

Sages—from the Orient far—
    Gazing on the azure dome,
Saw a strange—a wondrous star
    Luring them away from home ;

For it spake of One who came
To fulfill the hopes of old,
What the Seers in vision claim,
What the prophets had foretold.

In the clear nocturnal sky
Still they saw the triple star,
Shining in its sphere so high,
Shining near and shining far;
Dreams of ancient visions came
Floating on the midnight air,
Kindling in their hearts a flame
Pure and lofty—bright and fair!

Hasting they—the mystic three—
Magi high in story famed,
Came the wond rous child to see,
Child in vision Jesus named;
When the promised babe was born,
Born a king in Bethlehem,
On that fair and brightest morn
Came the Orient sons of Shem!

Joyous, bright, the Magi came,
Came, in eager haste, to seek—
Seek Him of the mystic name,
Born a king, so mild and meek;
"In the East, His star we've seen—
Seen it brilliant, seen it dim;
Guided by the radiant sheen,
We have come to worship Him!"

Vexed, alarmed, the tyrant king,
Greatly moved, the story hears,
Learned Rabbies doth he bring
To allay his doubts and fears;

And of them doth now demand
   Where Messiah should be born ;
" Here," say they—" in Judah-land,
   Blessed now, tho' erst forlorn !"

Then the despot—greatly ired—
   Called the Magi whom he feared,
Earnestly of them inquired
   When the mystic star appeared ;
" Go"—saith he—"to Bethlehem,
   Seek the wond rous child and bring
Word to me in haste again—
   I, too, would adore the king."

When his wish the Magi heard,
Heard the crafty tyrant's word,
   Hastily they sped their way ;
And the star, which they had seen
In the Orient sky serene,
Went before them till it came
Standing o'er the spot—the same
   Where the infant Saviour lay !

Fairly now the house within,
   They with Mary see the child,
Bending low, they worship Him,
   Worship Christ—the meek, the mild ;
And, their treasures op'ning. wide,
   Rarest gifts of gold they bring,
Frankincense and myrrh beside
   Offer they to Christ—their king !

Once their willing service done,
   Service rendered to their Lord,
Homeward haste they, and anon
   God doth kindly aid afford—

Warns them Herod not to see,
Homeward go another way;
Heeding, they the tyrant flee,
Glad—the voice of God obey!

Grateful for this help divine,
They with joy their steps retrace;
Still the mystic star doth shine,
Shines effulgent in its place;
Guided by His light serene,
Err they not, nor aimless roam;
Fended 'neath the radiant sheen,
They in safety reach their home!

SLAUGHTER OF THE INNOCENTS.

Heard ye, elate, th' enrapt'ring strains
Erst sweeping o'er Judea's plains,
In sweet celestial lays?
They were the songs of angels bright
Rejoicing in the coming light—
The light of better days!

That joy is changed to tort'ring fears,
And eyes are moist with briny tears,
Which now in torrents fall;
And hearts, with gladness full of late,
Now drain the bitter cup of fate—
Of wormwood and of gall!

The Despot, by the wise men mocked,
Is mad with rage, and men are shocked
With horrid deeds of blood;
For, sending forth his servile hosts,
Of vict'ry o'er the weak he boasts,
Avenged in crimson flood!

Fulfilled is what the prophets spake,
In Rama all of grief partake—
   A plaintive voice is heard;
The voice of mourning, sad and deep,
For Rachel doth her children weep,
   And weeps with hope deferred!

O bloody scene! O cruel fate!
Where all was peace and joy of late,
   Now sorrow reigns supreme;
There lamentation loud and strong,
And mourning o'er the cruel wroug,
   Are found in their extreme!

The blood of infant martyrs shed,
In vengeance, thus, to slaughter led,
   No longer they are near;
Sweet Innocents in crowds are slain,
And comfort none doth now remain
   The smitten heart to cheer!

THE FLIGHT INTO EGYPT.

Rapture reigned in Judah, then,
   Joy the heaving bosom thrilled;
For the cherished hope of men,
   For the promise was fulfilled;
Yet the welkin, dank and dark,
   Presaged trouble—presaged pain.
And the prudent eye could mark
   Wrath-clouds gath'ring o'er the plain.

Scarce the Magi yet are gone,
When an Angel from above
Comes to Joseph—sad and lone—
In a dream, with words of love,
Saying : " rise, and take the child,
Child so tender—dear to thee—
With his mother meek and mild,
To the land of Egypt flee !

" There remain, till thee I bring
Word of comfort, word of joy ;
For the bloody tyrant-king
Seeks the infant to destroy.''
Going thence, in haste, he took
Mary with the babe divine ;
Glad, the tyrant's realm forsook,
Safety sought in foreign clime !

Stayed he in that land remote,
Sheltered by the arm divine,
Until God in judgment smote
Herod of the scheme malign ;
That the mystic word of old
Might receive its sense anon,
" Out of Egypt have I called,
Called my well-beloved Son."

Safe—protected were the three,
Aided still by might divine ;
From the dread of tyrants free,
Exiled, they do not repine ;
Once the tyrant dead and gone,
Joseph, now, no longer fears ;
For an Angel from the throne
To him in a dream appears.

"Hasten, rise"—the Angel said—
"Take the mother, take the child,
They who sought his life are dead,
  Homeward bear the meek, the mild."
Quickly, then, he rose and took
  Child and mother, calm, serene,
Glad, the land of Ham forsook,
  Came again to Palestine.

Tyrants new the sceptre bore,
  Evils feared he, serious, grave,
Would his safety risk no more,
  Would no more the perils brave;
Fearing he, and warned of God,
  Turned aside to Galilee,
Where he found a safe abode,
  Sheltered and from danger free.

In a city small and mean,
  Dwelt they—dwelt the sacred three;
Naz'reth—as in vision keen—
  Prophets saw their home should be;
And the mystic word, once more,
  In fulfillment now is seen;
Word in darkness veiled before—
  "He shall be a Nazarene."

O the bliss—the rapture sweet
  Nestling in the trusty heart,
When, submissive at His feet,
  In God's love we share a part!
Dangers tho', in countless hosts,
  Daily crowd around our path,
Each, in God, a vict'ry boasts
  O'er the cruel sons of wrath!

"FEAR NOT LITTLE FLOCK."

Ye friends of the Saviour,
  And friends of mankind,
Come let us endeavor
  With heart and with mind,
The God of all mercies,
  The God of all grace,
To serve and to honour,
  To love and to praise !

His goodness has kept us
  In days that are gone,
His grace will sustain us
  In time that's to come ;
This truth is so precious,
  This hope is so dear,
That, living or dying,
  We never shall fear !

The God that made heaven,
  The earth, and the seas,
Doth He not sustain them
  So long as He please ?
And why—so much favored,
  Should WE not confide
In Him who has made us
  And ALL things beside ?

" If you, that are evil,"
    The Lord doth inquire,
" Do grant to your children
    The gifts they desire ;
Much LESS will your Father,
    Whose dwelling's on high,
The things ye have need of
    To you e'er deny.

" The voice of the raven,
    That sails in the air,
Your Father in heaven
    With pity doth hear ;
With food He supplies them
    Tho' num'rous they he ;
But, O, ye distrustful,
    Much better are YE !

"And think of the lilies
    That grow in the field ;
They toil not—they spin not,
    Nor increase they yield ;
Yet God doth array them
    In robes that are gay ;
And why should less goodness
    To you, He display ?"

Then fear not, beloved,
    Nor faint on the road,
Since God will supply us
    With raiment and food ;
Come, let us take courage
    And hope for the day,
When Christ in His mercy,
    Shall call us away !

Yea, let us be constant,
Nor yield to dismay,
And God will in season,
His glory display ;
At length, from all sorrows
He'll free us, His blest,
And grant us an entrance
To non-ending rest !

DARE TO DO RIGHT.

God is faithful, just, and true,
And will kindly care for you—
Bravely, then, the right pursue,
As is due !

THE BEATITUDES.

Once, weary with the cares of earth,
' The Lord of life was found
Ensconsed upon the mountain side,
With multitudes around ;
And, gazing on the eager crowd,
Who craved the light above,
He oped His sacred lips, and spake
In words of purest love :

Lo, "blessed" they, the weary ones,
Whom earth unhappy calls ;
On them, in sweet and tender notes,
The "benediction" falls ;
They be the richest far on earth
That are in spirit poor ;
For theirs the heavn ly kingdom is,
And theirs for evermore.

Yea, " blessed" are the contrite ones,
　　The burthened souls that mourn ;
The Lord will hear their plaintive groans,
　　To joy their sadness turn ;
For, in the heaviug breast is fouud
　　A soil productive, pure,
And every grace shall there abound,
　　And joy divine be sure !

Supremely " blessed" are the meek,
　　Who, fearing God, obey—
And, longing for salvation, seek
　　To walk in wisdom's way ;
For they, the blessed heirs of life,
　　The sons of heav'nly birth,
Are made to share in present bliss,
　　Inheritors of earth !

And " blessed" are the famished ones,
　　That hunger and do thirst,
And "righteousness" in earnest seek,
　　And seek this blessing first ;
Yea, blessed are these weary ones,
　　As God their bliss hath willed,
For they, the poor and needy, shall
　　With joys divine be "filled."

And " blessed are the merciful,"
　　The tender and the kind—
The sympathising friends of all,
　　The lovers of mankind ;
For they, in darkest seasons found,
　　Iu anguish of the mind,
Shall, even then, in bliss abound,
　　Sweet mercy they shall find !

Thrice "blessed are the pure in heart,"
The faithful and the true,
Who long with all on earth to part,
And higher ends pursue ;
For they, in all that greets them here,
In earth and sea combined,
In forest, field, and sky, shall see
A God supremely kind !

And "blessed" they, who, hating strife,
The ways of peace pursue,
And, following thus the Prince of Life,
Are found to virtue true ;
Renewed in heart, the Holy one
Says ; "they shall all be mine,
Blest children of the living God,
And heirs of life divine."

And "blessed" they, the pure and good,
The righteous and the just—
With every gift of grace adorned,
And free from every lust ;
Who, for their goodness, suffer wrath
And persecutions dire ;
For theirs are joy and heav'nly bliss,
Such as the saints desire !

And chiefly ye, the friends of truth,
Enlightened from on high,
Who, faithful to your Sov'reign Lord,
Proclaim Him far and nigh ;
Supremely "blessed" are ye just,
That goodness still pursue,
Tho' by the wicked world arraigned
For what is good and true.

"Rejoice, and be exceeding glad,"
Ye servants of the Lord—
Triumphant lift your heads on high,
"For great is your reward;"
For so the ancient prophets fared,
The faithful and the true;
Whom wicked men did persecute,
With vengeance did pursue!

LOVE YOUR HOME.

Once the soul, in thought estranged,
Frets in discontent at home,
Soon it, then—all things arranged—
Longs in distant lands to roam!

AROUND THE ALTAR TWINING.

Around the altar twining
Affections warm and pure,
In faith and love combining,
The crown of life secure;
Nor fear nor danger heeding,
The heart, thus firm and strong,
Tho' wily lusts are pleading,
Instinctive shuns the wrong.

Around the altar twining
Affections warm and pure,
In light and beauty shining,
To life and bliss allure;
The Lord, the mighty, shielding
His children 'neath His arm,
Nor to the tempter yielding,
Preserves them free from harm.

Around the altar twining
Affections warm and pure,
On virtue still reclining,
Of radiant glory sure ;
O happy they, who, hoping
In God, the mighty Lord,
With hostile forces coping,
Secure the great reward.

Around the altar twining
Affections warm and pure,
The trusty heart refining,
A blissful hope insure ;
Hence, happily reposing
On God in fiercest strife,
The soul itself composing,
Awaits eternal life !

THE LAST SUPPER.

The sun went down, that festal eve,
With gold and crimson in the sky,
And no one could, in fact, believe,
The tragic scenes that lay so nigh ;
The Master, in that upper room—
Convened with friends—once more at least,
Would, prior to his final doom,
With them observe the pascal feast !

While seated round the festive board,
He took the bread, and blessed, and brake,
" Take—'tis my body, broke for you,
This eat in mind of me"—He spake ;

Then took the cup, and, blessing, said
 " Drink ye, my friends, drink all of this,
This is my blood for sinners shed,
 'Tis life to you—'tis endless bliss !"

O joyous feast ! O blessed scene !
 What matchless grace to mortals shown ;
Such kindness ne'er before was seen,
 Such boundless love was never known ;
'Tis Jesus bringing life and peace,
 And pledging men sweet joys above ;
Then hasten. mortals, to receive
 These tokens of His dying love !

GATHERING IN THE ROSE-BUDS.

Little " beauties," scarcely born,
Basking in the dew of morn,
Tiny Rose-buds, sweet and fair,
Breathing in the balmy air,
From the stem so rudely torn,
Hapless seem and quite forlorn ;
Yet by fairy hands are brought,
Set in vases chastely wrought !

Placed upon the mantel fair,
Where, immersed in perfumed air,
Gently swelling, they expand
Into roses sweetly grand ;
In the night and thro' the day,
Fragrance now exhaling, they
Grandly thus the parlor grace,
Lovely, charming—just in place !

So the little wand'rers gay,
Cast upon Life's thorny way,
Here and there are ling'ring found,
Weary, way-worn, homeward bound ;
Loveliest, fairest of them all,
Gently doth the Master call
Up to yonder worlds above,
Full of beauty—full of love !

Hearts are saddened here below,
Bitter tears are caused to flow ;
Every earthly joy seems gone,
And the weary weep alone ;
But their joy, awhile restrained,
'Mid the losses here sustained,
Soon, in fuller measure giv'n,
Sweeter shall be found in heav'n !

Parents—mourning babes removed,
Treasures once so dearly loved—
Deeming all earth's pleasures gone,
Nothing left but tears alone—
Deem ye life all dark and drear,
With no ray of hope to cheer?
Bleeding hearts, with anguish riv'n,
Lo ! your babes are saved in heav'n !

Sweet the joy that hope doth give,
Children dying, still do live—
Happier far in realms above,
Bathing there in seas of love ;
Waiting, free from care and fear,
For the loved ones struggling here ;
Soon their bliss ye, too, shall share
In those mansions bright and fair !

THE HAPPY CHOICE.

I ask not for RICHES,
  Which cannot secure
A crown that is fadeless,
  Nor joys that are pure;
I ask but those riches,
  From virtue that 'rise,
The smiles of my Saviour,
  The pearl of great price!

I ask not for BEAUTY,
  This soon shall decay,
And leave me to linger
  'Mid shame and dismay;
I ask not such beauty,
  I seek but to find
The FAIREST in Nature,
  The beauty of mind!

I ask not for PLEASURES,
  From Nature that spring;
Like vapors they vanish,
  And leave but a sting;
I ask but those pleasures
  In death that endure,
Produced by the spirit,
  Sweet, lovely, and pure!

I ask not for POWER,
So eagerly sought,
With pain it is coupled,
With danger 'tis fraught;
I ask but for power
My spirit to rule,
Its passions to govern,
Its fears to control!

I ask not for FAVOR,
'Mong mortals below;
The good that is lasting,
They cannot bestow;
I ask but for favor,
With Thee, O Most High;
In weakness defend me,
In danger be nigh!

I ask not for HONOR,
The charm of mankiud;
The flesh tho' it pleases,
It poisons the mind;
I ask but for honor,
In Jesus my Lord,
The pledge of his pardon,
The seal of His blood!

I ask not for WISDOM
To earth that's confined;
With sin it is mingled,
With falsehood combined;
I ask but for wisdom
My duties to scan,
And render them daily
To God and to man!

I ask not for GLORY
    By conquest attained ;
With tears it is purchased,
    With blood it is stained ;
I ask but THIS glory—
    My name to survive
In Heaven's fair ledger,
    The Lamb's book of Life !

"THOU ART SO SWEET."

These were the dying words of a young lady, who, when no longer
able to speak aloud, continued to magnify the rich grace of God, in
Christ,—her tongue silently going through the motion—Thou art so
sweet—Thou art so sweet, until her spirit passed gently over into the
land of the blest.

Thou art so sweet !
When Nature's night so dark and drear,
By grace dispelled, did disappear,
And skies became all bright and clear,
Surprised, I sung—Thou art so sweet !

Thou art so sweet !
Ah ! since each day Thy grace I feel,
As near Thy throne I joyful kneel,
And Thou thyself dost there reveal,
I'll sing, I'll sing—Thou art so sweet !

Thou art so sweet !
At morn—when all so lovely seems,
The sun displays his radiant beams,
And air with choicest music teems,
I'll sing aloud—Thou art so sweet !

Thou art so sweet!
Thy name I'll praise at busy noon,
'Mid odors sweet and rosy bloom—
Thy word dispels the gath'ring gloom,
And sings my soul—Thou art so sweet!

Thou art so sweet!
At even-tide—all calm and still,
I lift mine eyes to Zion's hill,
And God my Saviour's with me still,
I'll sing with joy—Thou art so sweet!

Thou art so sweet!
At midnight, when my soul awakes
'Mid silent gloom and spreading shades,
And all before my vision fades—
I'll sing alone—Thou art so sweet!

Thou art so sweet!
While yet my blood so freely flows,
My soul with burning ardor glows,
And God His grace on me bestows—
I'll sing in youth—Thou art so sweet!

Thou art so sweet!
Yes, when I feel—reduced by age,
I soon must leave this earthly stage,
Let praise to God my soul engage,
While loud I sing—Thou art so sweet!

Thou art so sweet!
While life remains, my soul inspire,
O God, with love and sacred fire,
Let all my powers in haste conspire
To sing, enrapt—Thou art so sweet!

Thou art so sweet!
When sickness lays me on my bed,
And pains are o'er my body shed,
I'll lift my soul to Christ my Head,
And still sing on—Thou art so sweet!

Thou art so sweet!
When struggling in the arms of death,
When stops my pulse and fails my breath,
I'll rest secure in God, through faith,
And louder sing—Thou art so sweet!

Thou art so sweet!
Yes, when life's toilsome days are o'er,
And sin disturbs my soul no more,
I'll sing in strains unknown before,
My God, My God—Thou art so sweet!

TEKEL: OR, THE SINNER TESTED.

Thou art wanting!
Who is wanting?
He, whose thoughts from God estrange,
Whilst he blindly trusts to fate;
Though in death he seek a change,
Then, alas, 'twill be too late—
He is wanting,
Truly wanting!

Thou art wanting!
Who is wanting?
He who strives the world to please.
Seeks not heaven, shuns not hell,

Still lives on in thoughtless ease,
Oh ! his state is hard to tell !
    He is wanting,
    Sadly wanting !

    Thou art wanting !
    Who is wanting ?
He who serves not God, sincere,
    Nor obeys His mandates pure ;
He doth not the Lord revere,
    And to him destruction's sure.
        He is wanting,
        Surely wanting !

    Thou art wanting !
    Who is wanting ?
He, who makes not God his friend,
    Nor to Christ for safety flees ;
But lives thoughtless to his end,
    Till at length his doom he sees—
        He is wanting,
        Ever wanting !

    Thou art wanting !
    Who is wanting ?
He, that, when the Lord shall come,
    To collect His jewels rare,
Finds for him there is no room,
    And sinks down to dark despair—
        He is wanting,
        Greatly wanting !

    Thou art wanting,
    Who is wanting ?
He, who, when earth disappears,
    Finds himself engulfed in hell ;

Where must flow his bitter tears,
Where his sorrows still must swell—
He is wanting,
O, he's wanting!

COMFORTS OF RELIGION.

How sweet 'tis to mingle with saints of the Lord
To praise Him for mercies revealed in His Word;
Serenely look up to the place where He dwells
And draw from Him comfort as water from wells.

How sweet 'tis to linger beside the pure stream
Where pleasures forever, as truly 'twould seem,
Abide in their freshness to cheer the sad soul
And goodness and mercy encompass the whole.

How sweet to remember that all we possess
Results from His goodness, His mercy, and grace;
And feel the assurance, we need not despond
Since God is so gracious, so loving and fond.

How sweet to look forward, nor then be afraid
When death shall envelope the soul in its shade,
But lean with composure on Jesus' strong arm
Where pain cannot enter nor dangers alarm.

How sweet to look, also, beyond the thick gloom
That hides from the vision the sun-beams of noon,
There God and the Saviour forever compose
The spirit's sweet resting—its endless repose.

Aye, sweet from the valley of sorrows and tears
A home in the skies to the mourner appears;
He steadily looks to this mansion on high,
The pilgrim's dear Homestead reserved in the sky!

When sunk in affliction—in deepest distress—
And nothing remaineth to cheer and to bless,
'Tis THEN the lone pilgrim, tho' heaving a sigh,
Looks upward, and thinks of his portion on high!

THINE ALONE.

Yes, my Jesus, precious Saviour,
   I would yield myself to. Thee !
Seal this offering with Thy favor,
   And from sin my spirit free !
Thou hast saved me by Thy power
   From disease and early death,
And to Thee, in earnest prayer,
   I will spend my latest breath !

While my life and strength continue,
   I will seek Thy smiling face,
And for aye pursue that virtue
   Which is wrought alone by grace ;
Thou art worthy, O my Saviour,
   Thou art worthy to receive
Honor, glory, strength, and power,
   More than ever I can give !

O what mercy Thou hast shown me !
   O what joy and love and peace !
From destruction's dark forebodings
   Thou hast saved me by Thy grace.
Risen from the tomb with power,
   Thou hast burst the chains of death ;
Now to Thee, in grateful prayer,
   I will breathe my sweetest breath !

High ascended up to heaven—
Thou hast oped its pearly gates,
And redemption, dearly purchased,
On the weary pilgrim waits—
Waits to crown him with its graces,
And to free his captive soul ;
Jesus, I would sound Thy praises,
Thro' the earth from pole to pole !

Low before Thy gracious Presence
Bends my soul in humble prayer ;
There I find Thy pard'ning mercy,
And Thy goodness ever share ;
Lift upon my Spirit, Saviour,
Now alone Thy smiling face !
Let Thy grace, and truth, and power,
Let Thy love inspire my praise !

PRAISE THE LORD.

Earth's music sweet—of charming strain
And greens that deck the life-clad plain,
The scenes beneath, so passing fair,
And sounds that fill the balmy air,
      All—all unite,
      In gentle tide,
To swell and bear His praise along,
And chant to God a solemn song !
      Thus may you send,
      Dear Christian friend,
Sweet praise to God with ev'ry breath,
In sickness, health—in life and death ;
So shall you here secure His grace,
In Heaven enjoy His smiling face !

'TIS NOT IN VAIN; OR, THE CHRISTIAN LIFE.

'Tis not in vain!
Your tears that fall so thick and fast,
When day begins—when day is past,
Will bring to you relief at last—
   Your tears are not in vain!

'Tis not in vain!
Some soul among that happy band,
Who 'round the throne immortal stand,
May bless you when at God's right hand—
   Your work is not in vain!

'Tis not in vain!
Here lead a life of active faith,
And when you pass the gates of death,
Immortal bloom your brow shall wreath
   Your faith is not in vain!

'Tis not in vain!
Your hope, so constant, firm, and pure,
When life is past shall still endure,
And joy and peace beyond secure—
   Your hope is not in vain!

'Tis not in vain!
Your life here spent in faith and love,
With meekness tempered like a dove,
Shall bloom in endless spring above—
   Your life is not in vain!

'Tis not in vain!
The way to God seems dark and strait,
It leads, alas, thro' deaths thick shade.
But death to you is heaven's gate,
　　Your death is not in vain!

THE CHRISTIAN'S INHERITANCE.

Christian! view thy vast possessions,
　　Lo! the world is all thine own!
Thine the earth on which thou dwellest,
　　Thine the seas and thine alone.
Christian! lift thine eyes to heaven,
　　See the hosts yon skies display!
Radiant orbs, with glory beaming,
　　Thine, and thine alone are they!

Lo! the woodland's waving foliage,
　　And the mead's enchanting looks,
Lo! the ocean's surging billows,
　　And the songs of purling brooks,
Lo! the day's resplendent brightness,
　　And the night's secluding shades,
All unite to swell the gladness,
　　Which thy raptured soul pervades!

Hark! what soft, melodious breathings,
　　Float upon the morning breeze,
Sweetest perfumes, rich, enchanting,
　　Mingling, fill the air with these!
Saint! the songsters' lovely anthems,
　　And the flow'rets' charming hue—
All conspire to breathe thee solace,
　　All are here to comfort you!

Lo! the summer's golden harvest,
  Autumn scenes so passing fair—
Lo! the beasts that roam the forest,
  And the birds that sail the air—
Diverse hosts that tread the mountains,
  Finny tribes that scud the main,
All shall cheer the Christian's dwelling,
  All shall be the Christian's gain!

Nature yields thee vast possessions,
  Blessings thou hast largely shared;
But the richest of those blessings,
  Are but small with these compared;
Christ has died—the blessed Saviour,
  He has saved thy soul from hell!
Christ has risen—lo! in heaven,
  Thou shalt with Him ever dwell!

Jesus, raised to highest heaven,
  Now is seated on the throne;
And His Spirit, freely given.
  Kindly cheers thee, pilgrim lone,
And, at length, with peerless beauty,
  Will adorn thy rescued soul—
Christian! spread thy Saviour's praises,
  All is thine from pole to pole!

PRAISE IN NATURE.

Hark! The spring birds, near me singing,
  Fill the air with music sweet,
And—the echoes sweetly ringing—
  Glad the cheerful songs repeat!

Breezes o'er the earth are sweeping,
Which enhance its beauty still,
Cheer the pilgrim, weary, weeping,
And with joy ecstatic fill!

Flow'rets sweet, in sun-light basking,
Round me choicest fragrance pour,
Beauty, grace, and joy combining,
Cause my spirit to adore!

Nature, O, 'tis sweet and charming,
Clear and bright the fairy scene;
Forests decked with richest foliage,
Meadows robed in living green!

While these scenes, so fair and lovely,
Stand before my ravished eyes,
I would raise my soul delighted—
All-enraptured, to the skies!

I would bear my humble portion
In this song of heart felt praise,
And, with grateful soul adoring,
Now my voice with Nature raise!

CONTRAST IN DEATH.

THE SINNER.

Stretched on his pillowed couch the sinner lies;
His frame is racked with fell and keen disease
Which slowly works within—his eyes are sunk,
And pale his face. His languid looks show marks
Of life-consuming, dread disease at work—
His death is nigh, and sad the sinner's fate!
He looks; the world is fading from his dim,
Distorted vision; and a strange-toned voice

Of fearful import, falls upon his ear
And fills his soul with horror and dismay!
He looks again ; and finds his doom is fixed ;
The long probation past ; and all his strength,
His health, his life, he sees, in vain are spent.
He weeps.   His spirit once so stout, now quails ;
And trembling seizes on his frame !   He halts—
He thinks of time, but time no more is his ;
His trust is gone—the earth on which reposed
His fondest hopes.   The jests of sinners, now,
No more can ease his troubled mind, or bring
Composure to his soul with horrors deep
And dark forebodings filled.   Despair invades
His faltering heart—his hopes of life are fled,
And all is dark.   A world unknown now breaks
Upon his view.   The die, for him, is cast !
He sighs.   The scenes, his high-wrought fancy paints.
Are fearful, dark—of horror full and dread !
Fresh tortures still his soul invade, and sink
It deeper into woe extreme !   He dreads ;
He quakes.   His frame is tossed in anguish deep—
Consumed with burning wrath.   He cries to God
For mercy—O, 'tis mercy now he wants !
But, ah ! it is too late !   He cries once more—
O Heaven, save ! my spirit save, O God !
But no ! 'tis lost !—Ah, lost—forever lost !
Yet mercy !—no, 'tis gone !   I have destroyed,
Thro' sin destroyed my soul—my wretched soul !

THE SAINT.

The Christian led a life of faith and hope,
Of love and kindness oft to sinners shown ;
A life of suff'ring great, and deep distress !
And oft he felt the sting of keen reproach,
And darts of envy hurled to pierce his soul !
Yet, tho' he felt these poisoned arrows' stings,

He lived a happy man—possessed of peace.
And, now, this Christian, laid on death's cold bed,
Rejoices—not in wealth, or fame, or pow'r,
Nor aught by earth bestowed, but in his faith
And hope, and prospects bright of future bliss.
His mind is calm. His happy soul is rapt
In meditation sweet; and heav'nly peace
Sits on his countenance! He gently smiles,
And lifts his soul to God in praise and pray'r.
He knows full well his hope is fixed on high,
Where God in glory dwells—where Jesus reigns;
Where angels join, and saints, to praise the Lamb,
And raise, in everlasting songs of joy,
His glory high! The saint can well rejoice!
He calls to mind his life of faith and love,
His life of earnest pray'rs, and frequent tears
O'er sinners shed—his midnight watchings,
And kindly deeds bestowed on men of rank
Both high and low—bestowed on some whose hearts
Were steeped in sin, and filled with burning rage;
And on the meek and contrite ones, who lived,
And prayed, and wept, and ate their bread in tears;
Thus on the good and bad, alike, he smiled.
These deeds he calls to mind; and, O, the peace
Which they afford, no heart but his can tell!
In death's cold arms he feels supremely safe,
And lifts, in grateful strains, his soul to God.
Ah! he knows his Maker lives and watches
O'er his life with tender care. Confidence,
That priceless gift of God, dwells in his heart,
And spreads a calm composure o'er his face.
His soul is full of joy divine and peace;
Gently he sinks to rest. His thoughts now fixed
On future bliss, he thus exclaims: "Oh death,
Where is thy sting! thy victory, where, O grave!"

TRIUMPHS OF THE GOSPEL.

Lo! the Saviour's blood-stained banner
  Poised to catch the gentle breeze,
O'er th' extended range of mortals,
  Spreads its folds in joy and peace ;
They, who grope in midnight darkness,
  And in shades of deepest gloom,
Soon shall see the Gospel's brightness,
  And enjoy its precious boon !

We have felt its quick'ning power,
  We enjoy its precious grace—
Lo! its beams are spreading wider,
  Soon will touch at ev'ry place ;
Distant lands the sounds are catching,
  Sounds of joyous, happy news ;
And the echoes, swift rehearsing,
  Further still the light diffuse !

See, the West is raising higher
  Still the gently waving flag ;
And the East, in earnest prayer,
  Follows up the golden track ;
Isles are hast'ning to receive Him,
  Christ—the source of life and peace,
While the Gospel's living heralds
  Haste poor pris'ners to release !

Nations, sleeping, wrapped in darkness,
  From their slumb'ring state awake :
While the ancient forms of worship
  Deeply to their centre shake ;
Earth and hell, their firmness yielding,
  Soon the Gospel shall confess,
And the fruits of grace redeeming,
  Will the distant nations bless!

Where those proud, majestic rivers,
  Rolling swift in mighty flood,
Bear to seas their turgid waters,
  Crimsoned deep with human blood—
There shall glide the silv'ry streamlets,
  Bearing on their bosom peace—
There shall love, and joy, and gladness,
  Bless mankind, with gospel grace !

Where dark scenes of horror triumph,
  There shall stand the Saviour's cross ;
What before their gain they counted,
  Men shall count their greatest loss ;
And the world shall bring its honors,
  Near the cross shall lay them down ;
Raise to God their glad Hosannas,
  And with praise their Saviour crown !

CARRIER'S ADDRESS.

HAIL PATRONS, FRIENDS, THE CARRIER-BOY
HEALTH WISHES YOU, AND PEACE, AND JOY !

Good News I bring—an extra sheet,
  As oft I did through snow and sleet ;
'Tis kindly meant, tho' rather stern,
  As you will by experience learn.

Time was, when most, ye know, the aged spake,
But now-a-days the young their places take ;
And why not so ?   I here would humbly ask.
'Tis surely not of all the heaviest task ?—
And, since in wit, the young their seniors beat,
Why should the TONGUE submit to base defeat ?
My majors, then, stand back—just hear me talk,
Why not ? Sure I'm big—can—already walk !

Another year, I need not say, is flown—
FOOLS only tell what is already known.
My story is but brief, and briefly told,
Some new things tho' it tells, and some things old.
Depend on it, I shall not speak in vain,
Or, if I do, you have yourself to blame ;
Though but a lad, you see, a stripling youth,
My song, be sure, contains some precious truth.

The globose earth stands still, some people say,
And round it sweeps the burning sun each day—
High o'er us stretched, the wide expansive blue
Unaltered meets, each day, our steady view—
While yonder stars like trembling lights are hung
Deep in the clouds—the azure sky along—
And distant far, in shining worlds unknown,
Majestic reigns JEHOVAH—God alone !

" This doctrine's false," the lynx-eyed Seer exclaims,
" The earth revolves, and fixed the sun remains—
Thro' vasty space the stars their courses run,
And cheerful move their centre 'round—the sun."
This sure seems true—the OTHER seems like truth,
But which is right, 'tis hard to say for youth ;
To know is good—but not, is sure no crime,
Since we but wish to sing the course of time.

Time moves; but how is not so easy shown—
As moments come, the moments past are gone.
Oh!—simple quite this truth, you may declare;
Perhaps!—but, reader, know a myst'ry's there!
God's ways are deep. Time is—a truth sublime,
Yet time is changed to that which is not time.
Still, since we cannot grasp the slippery how,
We must not therefore waste the precious NOW!

Time moves we say: and, if IT change, then we,
Since we but live in time——eternity?—
Tremendous tho't! so great, so vast our doom!
Ah! whither going then—whence are we come?
Tossed from the hand of God, so pure, so good,
High, o'er creation chief, our father stood!
All Nature smiled—and lovely Eden trod
The man, deep on him stamped the image—God!

The tempter came—his subtle schemes applied,
Our father sinned. He fell, and falling died;
'Tis all we know, though speculation sought,
Still seeks to know, what far transcends all thought.
Yet, here it stands—its sad effects we know,
And, knowing, should avoid the curse—the woe!
'Tis wisdom to escape while yet we may—
Descending thunderbolts will have their way!

And how escape? Can I yet flee the rod?
And, flying, shun the burning eye of God?
See there, on yonder wall the gleaming sword
The trembling sinner warns to fear the Lord!
Alas! where flow'rets grew, sad Eden mourns,
And, lo! the blushing rose 'mid prickly thorns!
Sad change! yet, 'neath the earth-encircling shroud
Some hope-beams softly tinge the distant cloud!

The curse was scarce pronounced, when promised stood
A Saviour there—the pledge of future good!
Tho' time moved slowly on, each circling year,
Rehearsing, sang the promised day more near.
Time passed. At length the joyful period came,
And angels sang, and men, the Saviour's name!
He lived and died; His bloody cross now stands
The joy of Shem—the hope of other lands!

"Go, preach the Gospel," now the record runs,
" Whoe'er believes is safe—condemned who shuns."
But how shall they, who have not heard, believe?
And hear?—unless the Word they first receive?
By hearing then comes faith; and hearing how?
A preached Gospel by!—What duty now?
To make His counsels known—His firm decree:
"Come weary souls, I save—come unto me."

And how? No MATTER how—in various ways:
The pulpit, book, and sheet—each truth displays.
The quantum though we can't define exact,
'Tis deemed but just to state the simple fact.
The object sought, by diverse means we reach,
Myself may write—my friend prefer to preach,
Men differ, thus, in taste—just as in looks,
Fair speeches charm the one, another books?

Means vary then—ONE STORY all rehearse!
Truth speaks—the gloomy shades of night disperse.
Dominions, trembling, fall—dark systems cease,
And on their ruins, lo! the tents of Peace!
JEHOVAH reigns; and judgment now assigns
To each his doom—the end of God's designs:
And earth redeemed, and heaven, hell, combine
In triumph, thus, to close the course of time!

And how ?—we answered thus : " In various ways !
The pulpit, book, and sheet—each truth displays."
And here I, too, would now the chance embrace,
My merits thus in proper light to place—
'Tis not a pleasant task ; but who can blame,
If, brief, I modestly advance my claim ?
I'm sure—this is quite common now-a-days—
Each champion sounds his own peculiar praise !

My labors, though but few, are not so small ;
At many a door, I made my weekly call—
From many a flow'r I sipped the nectar sweet,
And laid it humbly at my Patrons' feet—
Good news at home, as well as news abroad,
I, modest, told in child-like fear of God—
And many a heart with anguish sore distrest,
I solaced oft, and oft the mourner blessed.

'Tis true, the wrath-cloud moved our heads above,
And much obscured sometimes the rules of love ;
Tho' thunders rolled, and lightnings wounded some,
The storm is o'er—a cheering calm has come.
On yonder cloud, the rain-bow's varied hues,
Sweet peace proclaim—a year of happy News.
Here stay my song—I lay mine honors down,
Join, angels, men, the God of Peace to crown !

BARTIMEUS : OR, JESUS AND THE BLIND MAN

Close by the way the blind man sat,
  And mourned his cruel fate ;
Requesting alms of those who passed
  And saw his sad estate :—
He sat and mused within his heart,
  How he should spend the day ;

When, lo! a large and num'rous host
　Came passing by that way—
He raised his head and gently asked :
　" Who comes along the road ?"
When from the crowd he heard a voice,
　Which said—" The Son of God!"
His heart was sad, and full his soul,
　He longed this man to see—
" Thou Son of David," loud he cried,
　" Have mercy, Lord, on me."
The thoughtless crowd his prayer heard
　And bade him stop his plea ;
But Christ rebuked them, and exclaimed
　"Come, bring this man to me—
I love to hear poor sinner cry,
　Nor will their suit disdain ;
For this I left the vaulted sky,
　For this on earth remain !"
His follow'rs feel the keen rebuke,
　And quick his word obey;
They bring before the Saviour's feet,
　The man without delay.
" What wilt thou," said the Saviour kind,
　" That I for you should do—
I came to make poor sinners whole,
　Shall, likewise, I heal you?
Now, when the beggar heard this speech,
　He felt his soul rejoice,
And ventured, thus, in humble strain,
　To raise his falt'ring voice—
" I wish, dear Lord, that thro' Thy word
　I may receive my sight;
Thus would I own Thee Sov'reign Lord,
　And in Thy name delight."
The Saviour, touched, in love responds—

" Receive thy sight," He saith ;
" I would not keep thee in suspense,
    Thou art made whole by faith."
Soon as the suppliant heard Him speak,
    His eye-sight was restored ;
And raising, now, his ravished eyes,
    The Saviour he adored—
And all the crowd, astonished much,
    Now spread His fame abroad ;
Raised high their glad and joyous songs,
    And praised the Sov'reign God !
And, now, ye sinners poor and blind,
    Lend to my voice an ear ;
And while I freely speak my thoughts,
    My counsels may you hear—
You know our Race in sin is steeped,
    By nature we are blind—
A darkness worse than this man felt,
    Rests on the human mind ;—
And should not YOU to Jesus cry,
    And ask His pard'ning grace ?
Thus only shall you e'er succeed,
    To win His smiling face.
But since we are so much defiled,
    So full of sin and shame,
Dare we approach His mercy-seat,
    Or trust the Saviour's name ?—
Yes, you may come and seek His grace,
    And in His name confide ;
His grace will cleanse your foulest guilt,
    His name your sins will hide.
What tho' your sin and guilt combined,
    Should form a purple flood—
There's mercy in the Saviour's name,
    There's pardon in His blood !

GRATITUDE.

Go—view the mighty rivers—
Go—view the purling brooks,
While gently they are dancing
Along the rocky nooks ;
They gather still their waters
From mountain and from plain ;
Then, with increased volume,
Return them to the main !

Go—view the plant so tender,
So charming and so fair ;
From earth it gathers moisture,
Inhales the balmy air ;
Then lovely stands it blooming,
Sweet odors sends abroad ;
Its leaflets, now descending,
Enrich the lowly sod !

Go—view the sportive insect,
Now glist'ning in the sun ;
Its life is but a shadow,
Its race as soon is run ;
And yet this little sporter,
May teach a lesson rare ;
For, lo ! its failing parent
It feeds with tender care !

Go, man, so proud and boasting,
   Go—view this humble train ;
Let Nature teach thee wisdom,
   Nor scorn its simple strain,
Though much to you inferior,
   Receive its precepts pure ;
Its teachings are substantial,
   Of this you may be sure !

Go—aid your needy neighbor,
   Go to his mean abode ;
Requite his love with favor,
   Commend his soul to God ;
Go—to your precious Saviour
   A song of triumph raise ;
Go—sing His saving power,
   And spread His lofty praise !

Go—render to your Maker,
   The love and honor due ;
'Twas He who gave you being,
   His hand created you ;
Why should not you be grateful,
   And serve the Lord in love?
Go—praise your God and Saviour,
   Who reigns and rules above !

LINES FOR AN ALBUM.

There is a FOUNT whose crystal flow
Spreads life and peace and joy below—
There is a SPOT whose charming sight
Resembles much the world of light—
There is a SONG whose winning strains
Lift up the soul to heaven's plains—

This song they raise,
In solemn praise,
When saints on earth unite to sing
The grace of their celestial king—
The CHURCH of Christ this SPOT we count
The BIBLE is that crystal FOUNT.
In life and death,
With gentle breath,
May e'er from you, dear Christian friend,
To Christ this charming SONG ascend—
Within His CHURCH still may you dwell,
Your BIBLE love, and search it well ;
So shall you HERE secure His grace,
In HEAVEN enjoy His smiling FACE !

THE RICH MAN AND LAZARUS.

There was a man in sumptuous style,
    Who fared from day to day ;
Whose gorgeous robes and linens fine
    His riches did display—
There was a beggar, poor, despised,
    Laid at the rich man's gate ;
His frame was weak and full of sores,
    And sad was his estate.
Poor Laz'rus craved the crumbs which fell
    From off the rich man's board,
Yet none but dogs, which licked his sores,
    Would friendly aid afford.
As time passed on the beggar died,
    On earth distrest, forlorn,
To Abr'ham's bosom swift his soul
    By angels bright was borne ;
The rich man died, and was interred,

In hell he raised his eyes,
And, tortured, saw on Abr'ham's breast,
Poor Laz'rus in the skies.
"O send him, Lord." now loud he cried,
His soul with anguish wrung—
" That he, with moistened finger-tip,
May cool my parched tongue ;
For, in this gulf of dark despair,
Still o'er my wretched soul,
The pains of hell and deepest woe
In flaming torrents roll !"
But Abr'ham said, " Remember, Son,
In life thou faredst well,
While Laz'rus felt misfortune's stings,
His sorrows who can tell ?
And now he feels sweet comfort here,
But thou the keenest pain,
And, thus, it shall for evermore
With him and you remain ;
Besides all this, a gulf is fixed,
That they, who would pass hence,
Are forced to yield their cherished hope,
Nor canst THOU e'er come thence."
" Send Laz'rus forth, I pray thee, then,
Quick to my father's house,
That from their deep and fatal sleep
My brethren he may 'rouse,
Lest they my fate should also share,
And come to this dread place,
Where torments keen and endless woes
Await our sinful race !"
But Abr'ham said in kindly tone,
" The prophets they have near,
And Moses, too, whom God hath sent,
These let your brethren hear."

The rich man, now, with anguish tossed,
And well-nigh in despair,
Lifts up to him once more his eyes,
And breathes this piteous pray'r:
" Nay, nay, my father Abr'ham, nay,
Some kindly message send;
For, if one from the DEAD should rise,
They will perchance repent!"
Still Abr'ham, true to his intent,
Would not his Lord betray,
But answered, thus, in faithful strain,
Nor sternly less did say:
" If they will not the prophets hear,
Nor Moses when he cries,
They would not listen, tho' one spake
Who from the dead did rise."
Thus closed the scene, and each remained
Where God His place assigned,
In heav'n the poor man was enthroned,
In hell the rich confined!

CHRISTIAN UNION—TO A FRIEND AT PARTING.

There is a strange—a mystic bond
That holds the human heart,
And breaketh not, tho' we be called .
On earth awhile to part:

It is that bond of quenchless love,
Which binds the happy souls above,
And sheds on man's deep-fallen race
A halo bright of matchless grace.
Where'er we be
On land or sea,

May still this bond 'tween us subsist,
In clearest light or darkest mist,
To keep our souls with sweet accord
United firm in Christ our Lord ;
  And on our way
  To endless day,
Whene'er we seek the Saviour's face,
Enjoy His love and sing His grace,
Then may we feel a brother's care,
And seek for him a blessing there.

Thus may we love each other still,
 While on Life's stormy sea ;
And each breathe out this tender pray'r,
 Dear friend, remember me !

THE SINNER SAVED.

The sinner lay upon his couch,
 With deep-dejected look ;
And, as he thought of future scenes,
 His soul with horror shook—
He raised his head, and deeply sighed,
 " Have mercy, Lord," he said,
" Nor let Thy vengeance, long deserved,
 Fall on my guilty head !

" Tho' long Thy grace I have despised,
 And so Thy love abused,
That, when Thy goodness I beheld,
 Thy mercy I refused ;
Yet, save me, Lord—with pity heed
 My groans, my sighs, my tears ; .
And with compassion now regard
 My terrors and my fears."

Thus prayed the sinner, poor, distrest,
And smitten deep with guilt,
When vengeance swept the sands away
On which his hopes were built ;.
But, as he prayed, distract with fears,
He heard a loving voice,
Which, while it filled his eyes with tears,
Did make his soul rejoice!

He heard—it was the voice of God,
Nor did its strains delay—
It bade him now with joyful haste
Wipe all his tears away ;
" For I," said He, " have seen and heard,
Above the starry skies,
Thy sighs and groans, thy sorrow deep,
Thy bitter tears and cries."

Oh ! how his happy soul rejoiced,
And how his heart did leap,
When, thus, in kind and friendly tones
He heard the Saviour speak ;
He raised his streaming eyes on high
And blessed His sacred Name,
While thro' the earth he spread abroad
The honors of the Lamb.

And sinners, now, he sought to teach
The goodness of the Lord,
How He had made His counsels known,
Sweet mercies in His word—
Where, for each sin of deepest dye,
A pardon rich is found,
A healing oil for ev'ry heart,
A balm for ev'ry wound.

The things he once so highly prized,
　And scenes he loved before,
Lost all their beauty to his soul,
　He felt their charms no more ;
But, in their stead, and nobler far
　The things of God appear ;
He loves to be where Christians meet,
　He longs their voice to hear.

And why should NOT the saint delight
　To linger where he hears
The voice that soothed his aching heart,
　And quite removed his fears ?
Why should not he delight to sing
　God's praise in joyful strain ?
For all things do him pleasure bring
　Whose soul is born again.

Then marvel not, ye mortals, steeped
　In sin and guilt and shame,
That he, who feels the Saviour's grace,
　Should love to sing His name ;
For tho' the earth should pass away,
　And stars should leave their train,
The saint, that's washed in Jesus' blood,
　In Jesus will remain !

WORTH OF THE BIBLE.

How perfect is Thy word, O Lord,
　Its doctrines how divine ;
It spreads salvation all abroad,
　And makes the nations Thine !

On every page stands forth Thy will,
　In characters of gold ;
Thy wonders—we can read them still,
　Tho' done in times of old.

Mercy and truth and love combined,
　To sinful men made known,
Here stand to welcome both refined
　And vulgar to Thy throne !

But, if we thus in goodness trust,
　On love and grace rely,
We also find our Maker just
　To let the wicked die !

He's sov'reign Lord of heav'n and earth,
　And all that's in them found ;
So doth He in His word declare,
　And in His works abound !

CHILD'S MORNING HYMN.

Soon as the dewy morn appears,
　My waking thoughts, ascend on high !
Far, far away my slavish fears,
　God gently calls—His grace is nigh !

Not earth shall fill my peaceful mind
　With inward terror or dismay—
In mercy's smiles my soul shall find
　The gentle beams of heav'nly day !

Away, ye sinful thoughts, depart
　Far as the East is from the West—
Earth's cares shall not engross my heart,
　Or e'er disturb my soul's sweet rest !

These sacred moments will I seize
  To fix my thoughts on things above ;
Dear Saviour, fill my soul with peace,
  My spirit sway with heavenly love !

So shall my feet delight to roam
  The path which Thou Thyself hast trod,
The road that leads me safely home,
  That brings me to my gracious God !

THE VICTOR SLAIN.

The drunkard lay beside the curb,
  His pulse was beating high ;
He felt a strangeness in his brains,
  But could not say just why ;
To speak the truth, his mind was gone,
  And reason's light had fled ;
Nor did he know that brick and stone
  Were now his only bed.

The boys were tripping up and down,
  And saw the drunkard lie,
But no one dared to speak a word,
  Or ventured to come nigh,
Till, all at once, a lad appeared
  More daring than the rest,
Who in this keen and simple strain
  The wretched man addressed :

" My friend, what mean you thus to lie,
  Exposed to vilest shame,
While men are passing thickly by
  And lisp thy former fame ?

Arise, and let thy country see
Thy name again restored
To what it was when soldiers brave
Thy presence nigh adored."

The people, now, with wonder struck,
Approached the dubious scene,
And asked with keen inquiring look
What once the man had been.
The youth resuming now his speech,
Tho' trembling and afraid,
Replied with more than usual skill,
As thus he briefly said :

" This man was not in former days
What he, alas, is now ;
For then a wreath of purest fame
Sat on his victor-brow ;
The seat of war his valor knew,
And glory crowned the man,
When thousands he to battle drew,
And led the conq'ring van.

" But now, alas, his fame is gone,
His mind is but a wreck ;
Nor can a power short of God's
The dread disaster check—
Yet, let the drunkard know your love,
Your sweet compassion share ;
Perhaps he may regain his strength,
Nor sink to dark despair."

The people heard this short harangue,
And praised the patriot lad,
While he rehearsed the hero's tale,
So tender and so sad.

And now their eyes are turned to him
  Who on the pavement lay,
That they might see if aught of fame
  His features did betray.

They saw still on his arched brow
  And o'er his furrowed face,
Of greatness many a signal mark,
  Of genius many a trace ;
And viewing now his lot so mean,
  The contrast was so great—
They could but shed a silent tear,
  And mourn his sad estate.

While thinking on the drunkard's lot,
  And on his former fame,
A feeling strange quick to the heart
  Of each spectator came.
They shrink, and as they sadly muse,
  Their feelings who can tell ?
The man sinks to a drunkard's grave,
  And to a drunkard's hell !

CHILD'S EVENING HYMN.

The mountain peaks, so green and gay,
  Bright gilded by the setting sun,
United sing the close of day,
  And show his wonted course is run !

The evening shades just now appear,
  And spread their dusky hues abroad ;
All Nature speaks His presence near,
  And chants a solemn lay to God !

Let me with Nature raise my voice
And sing to God a cheerful song ;
My soul in Him would e'er rejoice,
And still the Saviour's praise prolong !

These sacred moments well may serve
To raise my soul to worlds above ;
And, while I would Thy grace rehearse,
Fill Thou my soul with heav'nly love !

Let all my powers Thy name adore
And speak abroad Thy saving grace ;
Here may I feel Thy favor more,
In heaven enjoy Thy smiling face !

SWEET SURPRISE.

I passed by the church-door,
The building along,
And heard, all-enraptured,
A charming sweet song—
The song of the ransomed,
Ascending on high
From spirits where Jesus
With power was nigh !

Its soft-flowing cadence,
Its echoes so sweet,
Prevailed on my spirit
To seek the retreat ;
I entered the building,
And found on the spot,
Much people assembled
To worship their God !

Their songs of rejoicing—
　　Their sweet-sounding strain,
Bro't feelings oft-cherished
　　To mem'ry again—
I shared their rejoicings,
　　Their love in full tide,
As, cheerful in prayer,
　　I kneeled by their side !

Then, O, what sweet raptures,
　　My soul did enjoy,
While anthems were chanted,
　　Which angels employ !
There peace, far surpassing
　　What mind can conceive,
Distilled on my spirit,
　　Its pains to relieve !

The song of redemption,
　　The song of sweet praise,
Our spirits still lingered
　　In concert to raise ;
And, O, the sweet feelings,
　　The joys of the soul,
Like waves of the ocean
　　Continued to roll !

And, then, on the pinions
　　Of faith and of love,
Our spirits still mounted
　　To regions above—
Where, with the bright angels
　　All praising His name,
We still were rejoicing
　　In Jesus the Lamb !

Sweet, blissful devotion,
  So lofty and pure!
Thy scenes of rejoicing,
  Shall ever endure!
For, in that bright region,
  Where God doth abide,
This song of redemption
  Flows on in full tide!

THE SABBATH.

Lo! the Sabbath day is dawning,
  Christian, trim thy golden lamp!
Let its flame be brightly burning,
  Let it bear the royal stamp!
May not sin, thy mind diverting,
  E'er engross thy thoughts to-day;
Oh! attend the Saviour's warning,
  And give ear to what He'll say!

See, He comes to meet His people,
  Gath'ring round His sacred shrine;
There, before His altar kneeling,
  All shall taste His love divine!
Come then, Christians, hasten hither,
  Come prepared in heart and mind;
Here, to-day, by humbly seeking,
  All, who will, their God may find.

Let the day be with thee sacred,
  And thy thoughts be fixed above!
Seek thy Saviour's gracious presence,
  Seek His sweet and boundless love!

So the Sabbath thee shall comfort,
  Cheer thee on thy weary way—
Till, at length, in yonder mansions,
  Thou shalt spend au endless day!

INVOCATION.

Come, gracious Spirit, tune my heart,
  While I would sing Thy praise—
Come, and inspire my languid tongue,
  To heaven my feelings raise—
So shall I still Thy wonders sing,
And praise to God my Saviour bring!

E'en as the dawning day appears
  And spreads the shades of night,
So on this poor, benighted soul
  Shed beams of heavenly light—
O, let me feel Thy presence near,
No more let sin in me appear!

For, as the dew-drops gently fall
  Wide o'er the sterile ground,
And make its parch'd and desert soil
  In richest fruits abound—
So let Thy grace still life impart
To this my drear, my failing heart!

Yea, come, enrich me with Thy grace,
  And shed Thy love abroad;
So shall I early seek Thy face—
  Shall seek my gracious God;
Then, come, with beams of mercy shine
Upon this aching heart of mine!

STORM AT SEA.

Dark o'er the storm-tossed, spraying deep it hung,
A murky cloud with sportive lightning charged,
Displaying still its strange and varied scenes
Of light and darkness mixed. Silent it stood
As if it dared the boist'rous deep beneath ;
Anon, the coming storm, uptossing high,
Disturbed the wondrous, ever-shifting scene ;
Within the huge and strangely-poised cloud
The livid lightnings played. The rushing tide
Up-heaves the billowy, splashing deep beneath,
And surging wave on wave succeeds ; and, lo,
The ocean rocks. Deep sounds are heard around ;
And fragile barks, 'neath which the waters boil,
Are rudely tossed about ; and all is noise,
And tumult, with alarm. A brilliant flash
Of lightning blinds the eye, and strikes the soul
With dread. In zigzag line it darts athwart
The murky sky ; and, in the distance, there
Is heard the mutt'ring thunder ; loud peal to
Peal succeeds. The dark, cerule deep reflects
The brilliant lightning flash. The souls of men
Who on its bosom sail deep horror stirs ;
And trembling, now, they grasp the rocking ship
As o'er the hoist'rous deep it scuds. Despair—
Dark, stern, despair on ev'ry count'nance sits.
As eye meets eye, and ghastly visage looks
On face as grim, and quiv'ring lips reply

To quiv'ring lips—the trembling hand is seen
To clasp such trembling hand, and piteous groans
In other hearts such death-like groans awake,
And burning tears to tears of brine respond !
As scenes like these, confront the eye of man,
The sturdy soul shrinks back in horror deep,
And well-nigh yields to fate. Destruction e'en
And sudden death less dreaded are than they !
Scenes, such as these, do probe the hearts of men,
And show what are their hopes and aims beyond
The present world. The Christian, who has learned
To place his trust in things unseen, and seeks
In yonder world a life which fadeth not—
Who lays up treasures where no thief can come
And rob him of his wealth, rejoiceth then,
And hopes, anon, to see his Father's face.
But he, who lives a sinner, proud, and scorns
To bow before his Maker's throne, now feels
His vitals freeze with chill and deadly fears;
And on his scornful brow there sits enthroned
A desperation wild : While hell beneath
Him opens wide its jaws to circumvene
And lodge him in its fiery womb. Ah ! then
What horror fills his soul! He weeps, he mourns :
He calls for help. His heart, that earlier scorned
To show dependence on a higher Power,
And, thus, his Sovereign God acknowledge,
Now fails him ; and the frail and reeling bark
Doth witness scenes of earnest, piteous, pray'r.
His streaming eyes are raised to God ; and, on
That deck, beneath the expanded star-lit
Heavens, he humbly bends his knees. No more
Doth him the shame of man deter yielding
To his Maker, God, and rend'ring homage
To Him who rules in heav'n, on earth, in hell !

Thus on the troubled deep the lightnings play,
And thunders roll along the mantled sky,
While lawless storms upheave the watery deep
And toss the dashing spray. The massive ships,
Those monuments of human art and skill,
Are tossed upon the rough and foaming deep,
Till naught but sad and floating wrecks remain.
To those who sail upon the storm-tossed main
At such an hour, a scene like this displays
A spectacle at once sublime and grand !
ONE, indeed, looks on with sweet composure,
And feels a peace within before unknown ;
Beside him stands ANOTHER, filled wilh dread,
His guilty soul o'erwhelmed with fear of hell !·

SPRING.

Sweet Spring ! Thou com'st in such a lovely guise,
And in such beauties clad, that, spell-bound, we
Thy charms admire, and hail thee with delight !
Thou usher'st in thy reign with sweetest notes
And all-harmonious strains of warbling birds ;
The woods and hills are vocal with their songs,
Which, re-echoing, greet th' enraptured ear
Of such as roam these lone and charming wilds !

The bland, soft air of balmy morn is filled
With music sweet ; and evening zephyrs,
Gently whispering, speak their sad, pathetic
Tales of love, and o'er us waft sweet odors—
The fragrant breath of blooming trees exhaled ;
And sunny noon, alike with morn and eve,
Displays its charms. Aye, strangely pleasing scenes
Cheer night and day, while thou, sweet spring, art nigh!

No more stern winter seals the gurgling brooks—
The streamlets wild, from crystal bonds released,
Now nimbly dance full many a long. lone day,
In winding course, thro' verdant meads and dales ;
And, in the streams—the clear and rushing tide—
The num rous finny tribes now sportive play,
And nimbly dart along the silvery crest,
While on its bosom gleams the morning sun !

Oh ! how thy charms, sweet Spring, my soul elate,
And fill me with delight ! Ecstatic joys
Sweep o'er my ravished breast ; and lovely scenes
Of meadows. clothed in living green. and groves
With opening blooms of diverse tints adorned,
And charming music, from a thousand tongues,
In concert tuned, all strike mine eyes and ears,
And 'mind my soul of Heav'n's eternal spring !

Then hail, sweet Spring ! Suggestive of the dawn of life,
When from these earthly scenes my soul shall pass
To yonder lovelier, brighter, scenes on high !
Thou lead'st me back where erst the morning stars
In concert sang, and all the sons of God
Did shout for joy. Thy life-clad hills, so fair,
And newly-opening blooms remind me all
Of scenes like those of resurrection morn !

O Saint ! how will that morn of days, and spring
Of years, delight and charm thy ravished soul !
Delightful morn to thee ! The mellowed songs
Of angels pure and saints shall greet thine ear ;
And melting strains from golden harps, and tongues
With sacred fire touched, shall in thy bosom
Find an echo—a kindred cord, which shall
With rapture sweet and joy to them respond !

VISIONS OF HEAVEN.

Stern winter had vanished, so drear and so long,
And woodland and valley were vocal with song,
As down a lone meadow I pensively strayed
All-studded with flowers—in beauty arrayed.

Each object, encountered, seemed pleasant and new,
And exquisite beauties stood forth to my view;
All, all was so simple. so lovely and fair—
With Nature, so charming, O, what can compare?

The gay-dancing streamlet that flowed by my side
Made music so simple and free from all pride;
Its soft-flowing cadence—its echoes so sweet
Bro't scenes to remembrance with rapture replete.

I tho't of that music whose soft-flowing strains,
Distilling like dew-drops on Bethlehem's plains,
Gave "glory to God," and to mortals forlorn
Proclaimed the good news that a Saviour was born.

I thought of that moment when first on my view
Brake scenes of Redemption so rich and so new,
When Jesus, who saw me in gloominess grope,
Became to my spirit the "day-spring" of hope!

I thought of yon Temple—sweet portals of bliss—
And mansions we enter when called to leave this,
The Home of the pilgrim, once wearied below,
And oceans of pleasure unmingled with woe!

I tho't of that pureness—the sweetness and love,
The BEAUTY that reigns in the mansions above;
These visions—so lovely, so blissful, divine—
This beauty, dear reader, this sweetness, be thine !

ROSES ON A GRAVE.

Wherefore, Roses, do you bloom ?
Asks one trav'ling to the tomb ;
Therefore, stranger, that we cheer
Freely thee, while thou art here !

THE VOICE OF PRAISE.

I saw a little sportive bird
  Of golden plumage, fair,
Its sweeter notes of music heard
  Soft-floating on the air—
I saw, and flow'rs of various hue
  Bedecked the turf I trod,
And all, tho' silent, seemed to say
  Behold our Maker God !

I saw the crystal streamlet flow
  In playful mood along,
And from its simple music rose
  To God a grateful song—
I saw the starry hosts above
  Illume the dismal night,
And all their gentle raylets strove
  To praise th' Eternal Light !

I saw, and at Creation's head
  A loftier being stood,
Saw Man with far sublimer gifts,
  With nobler pow'rs endued ;
And shall not HE sincerely strive
  His silver voice to raise—
Look up to God with cheerful heart,
  And sing His endless praise ?

LOST AND SAVED.

The full-sail ship securely rode,
  Slow on the dancing main,
While sailors viewed, with cheerful eye,
  The beauteous marble plain ;
But soon a murky cloud appeared,
  Poised in the distant sky,
And as they watched, they trembling saw
  The gathering storm draw nigh.

The heavens, awhile before so bright,
  Now tinged with deepest gloom,
Presaged a storm that soon should rise
  And seal their threatened doom :
The boist'rous deep is tossed and torn,
  The sailing bark is checked—
The vessel breaks—the cargo sinks—
  The wretched crew is wrecked !

Yet many a one the danger braved,
  And, struggling with the tide,
Was from the angry waters saved,
  And saw the storm subside.

Thus, rescued from a watery grave,
    And safely brought to shore,
They praise Him who is strong to save,
    And laud Him evermore!

I, too, was once on board a ship,
    Stanch, sailing on the deep,
No gathering storm around me raged,
    To break my sinful sleep ;
The world I viewed with calm repose,
    Its pleasures I enjoyed—
No serious view of coming wrath,
    My busied thoughts employed.

Thus calmly on the storm-tossed deep,
    My bark securely rode,
While in the thickest gloom of night,
    My careless soul abode ;
But He, whose mercy I despised,
    Whose grace I thrust aside,
My fears alarmed, and kindly said :
    " Canst thou my wrath abide ?"

From that dread hour my fear increased,
    My feelings who could tell ?
From every hope my soul had ceased,
    And feared a dismal hell ;
The gathering storm drew nearer still,
    Its gloom obscured my path,
While o'er my soul suspended hung,
    The glittering sword of wrath !

My hopes are gone, and deep despair
    Invades my trembling soul ;
Above is wrath—beneath I see
    Hell's fiery billows roll—

But Jesus comes—His pity moves
As He my state beholds;
My cries He hears—within His arms,
His wand'ring child He folds—
A heav'nly peace my soul pervades,
No terrors are abroad—
My joy is full, since deep is hid
"My life with Christ in God."

JESUS ALL IN ALL.

Jesus! Name most dear to me,
Jesus! all that eye can see,
Jesus! all that heart can taste,
Jesus! Thou of all the best!

Jesus! Thou my daily food,
Jesus! Thou my only good,
Jesus! Thou my portion now,
Jesus! mine for ever Thou!

Jesus! Thee alone I seek,
Jesus! rapt of Thee I speak,
Jesus! Thee my Love I call,
Jesus! Thee my ALL IN ALL!

Jesus! Thee in health I love,
Jesus! Thee in sickness prove,
Jesus! Thee in life I own—
Jesus! Thee in death alone!

Jesus! when my life is o'er,
Jesus! when on Canaan's shore,
Jesus! when I'm safe at home,
Jesus! Thee I'll praise alone!

Jesus! when the skies have oped,
Jesus! when in glory robed,
Jesus! Thou my joy, my love,
Jesus! Life in REALMS ABOVE!

THE CHARMS OF RELIGION.

There's sweetness in the mellowed strains
    That strike the ear at break of day,
When Nature from her slumber wakes,
    And feathered warblers chant their lay!
But sweeter far that song so choice
    Which angels sang on Bethl'hem's plains,
And sweeter still my Saviour's voice
    Which now my beating heart enchains!

There's grandeur in the noon-day sun,
    And beauty in the moon's soft beams,
There's splendor in yon starry host,
    Whose brightness 'mid the darkness gleams;
But glorious more than mid-day sun,
    Than moon's soft beams more lovely far,
Much brighter than yon glittering host,
    Is He—my soul's bright morning star!

There's music in the gurgling brooks,
    And grandeur in the rushing tide;
Romantic scenes my vision meet
    On yon majestic mountain side;
But, high above those vaulted skies,
    Where suns in brightest glory shine.
Far nobler scenes attract mine eyes,
    There sits my Saviour all-divine!

There's magic in the world of thought,
And glory in the depths of mind,
There's pleasure in sweet friendship's smile,
And joy in converse with mankind;
But brighter, sweeter, is that world,
Whose beauties eye hath never seen,
Whose music ne'er has touched the ear,
Nor charms by heart conceived have been!

There's vastness in creation round,
And wisdom in the world displayed;
There's beauty in its life-clad plains
And trees in richest robes arrayed;
But, in yon world where Jesus reigns,
Far lovlier scenes attract my view,
There all is life, and love, and peace—
There all through endless ages new!

There's sweetness in the balmy morn,
And softness in the twilight gray,
There's quiet in the midnight gloom,
And charms are in the gleam of day;
But, O, ten thousand times more sweet,
More soft the dawn of that bright morn,
When I, 'mid sweet seraphic strains,
Shall to my Saviour's side be borne!

GLORY OF THE CROSS.

The cross! the cross! Stupendous theme,
So vast, so deep—profound abyss!
Deep as the utmost verge of hell,
And high as yonder world of bliss!
The vasty spheres that whirl in space,
And stars that burn in distance far,

Yon worlds unknown, no eye can trace,
  And suns and moons thy glory share!
Blest, bloody cross! Thrice dear to ME,
  On which my Saviour, Jesus, died;
Sweet, sacred cross! I gaze on thee,
  And, gazing, in that blood confide,
    Which seals my bliss,
  And yonder, in that "book of Life,"
    Records my name!

"WHERE ARE THEY?"

Say, where are they, the path who trod,
  That leads to Zion's hill—
Who with us praised their Saviour God,
  With voices soft and still?
O where are they, who, mourning sin
  With floods of burning tears,
Looked up to God, found solace there,
  A balm for all their fears?

Say, where are now those lovely bands
  Of Christians, young and old,
Whose cheerful hearts and beaming eyes,
  Their bliss—their fervor told?
Whose burning hearts and voices clear,
  In concert oft and sweet,
To God arose—to praise His Name,
  With joy and bliss replete!

Ah! tell me but where summer scenes,
  Where flow'rets bright and gay—
Whose fragrance sweet rejoiced the night,
  Whose beauty cheered the day—

Where they are gone, there too are those,
Of whom we now complain—
Their former joy—their bliss is gone—
Where pleasure was, is pain!

NEW-YEAR'S GREETING.

ALL HAIL! YE PATRONS, FIRM AND TRUE,
A " HAPPY" NEW-YEAR GREETETH YOU!

'Tis custom—and, I cannot say 'tis wrong
For Carrier-boys to sing a New-year's song ;
To greet their Patrons in appropriate lines,
And, with the new year, wish them easy times.
　　But hand me, first, a little "chink"—
　　I'm sure 'twill help my head to think ;
　　And—on receiving ready cash,
　　My pen will cut a finer—dash!
Alas! this vile begging! The "change" will appear,
'Tis shameful to doubt it—more shameful to fear ;
No man will, on " New-year's day," forfeit the joy
That flows from rewarding the dear "Carrier-boy."

'Tis not so small a "TASK," as school-boys say,
To write a NEW address, each New-year's day ;
The day indeed is new—or new in kind—
But so each OTHER day, if well defined.
Its special claim is this, as would appear,
'Tis "new," because it ushers in the year ;
And years compose the life-rule here below,
And seal our bliss, or doom to endless woe!

This special day—distinct from all beside,
To one grand purpose then may be applied ;
It constitutes—if I may thus define—
'Twixt year and year the separation-line.
The "old," stamped on Omniscience' book, remains,
By virtue marked—or by pollution's stains.
Untried—distinctly though within our view,
Stands the inviting, bright, and future new.

The day reviewed—its purposes defined,
And to each oue a solemn part assigned,
The query comes, and for the past demands
A strict and solemn answer at our hands :
The year—how was it spent ? its duties met ?
Doth its review occasion no "regret?"
Say, how has man been used ? how God adored ?
How sins confessed ? and mercy—how implored ?

I'm sure I brought—just as I brought before,
Last year, a weekly "message" to your door—
To suit the diverse tastes of many minds,
I brought delicious fruits of various kinds.
To cheer her sex, when summer days were long,
The gentle Western "muse" most sweetly sung ;
And when she ceased, another caught the fire,
And strikes, to this day, still her tuneful "lyre."

The "boiling springs," tho' now they've ceased to boil,
Some lengthy sheets dispatched, 'midst various toil ;
And e'en the Schuylkill hills their portion gave,
In cheerful rhyme—in "conversations" grave.
The frigid North, mild East, and distant West,
Each furnished some—good, better, some the best ;
And from the South, woe, woe, the fated dance !
Spake some one like—'twas not exactly "Lance."

Yet more. " My Study '—signed by " E. H. N."
Most brilliant pictures drew of various men ;
And brother " B."—but, lest I should forget,
I'll simply mention here that " X. Y. Z."—
And brother " B.," for young and old, I guess,
Each Monday morn dispatched a new "Address."
And " Vinet"—for, we deem it here in place—
And "Vinet" urged a steady "growth in grace.'

Sometimes, 'tis very true, a lance was broke,
And some may now regret what then they spoke.
So " Aleph's" pen involved a host in blame,
And " Alpha" censured him, to save his name.
For, sometime since, you know, a scourge appeared,
On polished canes, and specks, and partners " deared."
The scourge was felt, and raised a dreadful " storm,"
'Twas, therefore, best that "blame" disown in form !

And of " Germania's" sons—excuse the name,
Where words don't rhyme, the poet's not to blame,
One of Germania's sons a " picture" drew,
Somewhat too dark, it seems, for me and you.
But, pray, let's pass the matter off in sport,
And cross the blunders in his long " report ;"
For—as they say—he left his love behind,
And love, you know, 'is always painted " blind."

And, then that doctor—best suppress his name—
Some chance time still plays off his wonted game ;
Whilst sturdy " West," and Eastern critics join,
To pay the " scribbler" off in his own coin.
But cease this warlike strain—the work define
Which lies beyond the " separation' line—
This done—I'll close my dull, protracted song,
Which even now, I fear, is much too long.

And first of all—let each one now assist
To swell the coming year's subscription list.
Peruse my sheet—'twill much your joy enhance,
And always pay your " paper"—in advance !
Why˜so ?   What reason can there be assigned,
Why this injunction men should bear in mind ?
Precisely this—that, if they pay before,
They need not pay it when the year is o'er !

One other thing—-my notions please excuse,
One other thing I here would introduce,
The paper—mark it !—can't itself produce,
It needs assistance—-don't this aid refuse !
And, whilst to dictate we would not presume,
I would suggest—'twill save no little room—
To use not many words—do but express
Your finest thoughts, the rest let readers guess !

My work is done—my puzzling task performed,
The " noble" flattered, and the vicious scorned !
" What's writ, is writ"—the critic's scorn despite !
Though dull it be, or e'en insipid quite.
'Tis good enough—and this is all my joy—
'Tis good enough for me a " Carrier-boy."
A happy " New-year," Patrons, waits for you,
My song is o'er, except one word—Adieu !"

BLEST IN CHRIST.

Nor eye hath seen so fair a sight,
     Nor ear hath heard so sweet a sound,
Nor heart enjoyed such pure delight,
     As in my Saviour I have found.

On Him my brightest hopes repose,
And sweetly on His love I rest;
While He is near I fear no foes,
But in Him feel supremely blest.

'Tis Jesus—who, in Life, shall be
My hope, my joy, when sins prevail;
'Tis Jesus—who shall comfort me
When every earthly hope shall fail!

ACROSTIC—IMPROMPTU.

Much as of pleasant things we speak,
In sin such things we vainly seek—
Sin yields at best but terrene ease,
Seek not, then, here for solid peace!

Sad are the scenes, but seldom sweet,
Upon this earth we're called te meet;
Sad are its sorrows—sweet its joys,
And yet these last are empty toys;
Not on this earth, not in its scenes,
Not in its fond, its fairy dreams,
Are joys the truly wise esteems—
Earth yields us only pain!

Some seek, I know, their pleasures here,
Urged by their fancies—not by fear—
Lost to all virtue—who may tell
Their state so sad—not bliss, a hell?
Zion—be thou the Christian's joy!
Bound up in thee—without alloy—
Are pleasures found! Lone pilgrim, this,
Chief joy—be also thine, thy bliss—
Here found, thy joys remain!

THE CAGED DOVE.

SINGULAR.—Our friend Mr. E. B. Eichholtz, who is fond of birds, had a dove which exhibited a great aversion to its prison, and a strong desire to be free; its struggles were so continued and painful, that finally a feeling of compassion prevailed, and the gentle, cooing bird was set at liberty. and away it soared, away—away—with rapid wing. Three weeks or more elapsed, when Mr. E. was surprised, one morning, by a visit from a strange dove, which seemed to clamor for attention and a cage; a cage was given it, when lo, by certain unmistakable marks, Mr. E. knew it to be his quondam feathered pet, which had returned, wounded and weary, to be nursed. Some relentless sportsman had shot it; one leg was broken, and the bird was otherwise injured. It is now well and seems perfectly happy in its wire-wrought home. Here is food for thought and material for Poetry.—*Miners' Journal.*

In the wiry cage enclosed,
   Lonely sat the cooing dove,
Free, in groves no more reposed,
   Softly there to speak her love;
All her former joys debarred,
   Every scene she loved so well;
Who can paint her destine hard,
   Who the cheerless story tell?

Anxious round the cage she looked,
   Fondly hoping some relief—
Gladsome every hardship brooked,
   Gently breathed her tale of grief;
Still her every effort failed,
   She no friendly aid obtained—
Yet, at length, her suit prevailed,
   And her freedom she regained.

Quick her azure pinions poised,
  Swiftly through the air she flew,
Sought her love-companion host
  Where to nestle them she knew ;
Sweetly passed the time away,
  As she winged her joyous flight,
Wearied not by close of day—
  Rested not at dead of night.

But she found not those she loved,
  Saw no one she knew before—
Distant far her mates removed,
  Every scene seemed sad and sore ;
Fowlers, ranging o'er the plain,
  Cruel, gave an aching wound,
Lonely, racked with piercing pain,
  Where? O where, could rest be found ?

Like the imprisoned China-man,
  From his dungeon dark released,
Sought his lone retreat again,
  When he found his friends deceased ;
So the wand'ring dove—forlorn,
  To a friendless world consigned,
Doomed in freedom's range to mourn,
  Rather chose to be confined.

Sad, she turned from scenes abroad,
  Backward traced her wand'rings lone,
Guided by her unseen God,
  Safely reached her destined home,
Trembling, now, to fate resigned,
  Craved again admittance there—
Glad in cage to be confined,
  Seasons foul and seasons fair !

Shrewdly, brave, her cause she plead,
　　Frequent móved her body torn,
Showed her limbs of crimson red,
　　Hero-like, her state forlorn ;
Moving strains her master hail,
　　Gently flow her notes of love,
These, combined, on him prevail,
　　He receives the cooing dove !

Rescued from the fowler's rage,
　　Safely all her perils o'er—
Glad, she hails her wiry cage,
　　Freedom she esteems no more ;
Much by sad experience taught,
　　Humbled, now, content and meek,
That she once so eager sought,
　　She resolves no more to seek.

Every danger freedom wore,
　　Every pain she then endured,
Now she feels can harm no more,
　　In her wiry cage secured ;
Where, in sadness once confined,
　　Cherished tho' by hands of love,
There contented, blest, resigned,
　　Cheerful sits the cooing dove !

CHILD'S DEDICATION HYMN.

My Saviour—dearest to my heart,
Thou dost to me each good impart ;
Then why, O why, should I decline
And not myself to Thee resign !

Thou art the fountain of my life,
And I must not against Thee strive,
While Thou art holding out Thy hand
To lead me to that promised land!

Forbid it, Lord, that I should be
Ungrateful, and estranged from Thee;
Since Thou art willing to forgive,
And wouldst have me in glory live!

'Tis yonder that my home shall be
Through endless ages—blest in Thee;
'Tis yonder, I shall see my God
Now gracious in redeeming blood!

For didst not Thou, Almighty king,
Descend and us salvation bring?
Ah! Lord, 'tis mercy reigns on high,
This prompted Thee to come and die!

It was of love the Lord came down
And meekly bore the thorny crown,
That sinners might return to Him,
And be redeemed from death and sin.

Lord, I am Thine, I must confess,
Since Thou art ever kind to bless,
And pray Thee keep me in Thy fear,
Until the "Son of Man" appear.

To Thee I now resign my soul,
My future life do Thou control;
And while I live, I'll live to Thee,
Who Father, Son, and Spirit be!

LINES ON THE ABOVE.

Written when the shades of night,
Low'ring hung around my bed;

When my spirit deeply sighed
After Christ my living Head.

LINES TO A BEREAVED SISTER.

Written on the reception of a letter containing a notice of the death
of the third child of my sister—all of whom had died within the space
of a few years.

Parents sad—of peace bereft—
Scarce a comfort you is left;
Piercing, have successive darts
Entered deep your bleeding hearts;
Children, whom you dearly loved,
One by one have been removed!

Keenly were the pains it gave,
Felt, to see your first one's grave;
Scarce were healed the hearts it broke,
Ere you felt a second stroke;
Tears still brinier now are shed,
As one love-pledge more is fled!

Parents sad—I weep with you,
Feel your pangs—your sadness too;
I, who bear a brother's heart,
In your sadness share a part—
Weep with you, who justly weep,
Seek the comforts which you seek!

Oh! a balm for souls distrest,
Is a brother's feeling breast!
Know we but that those we love,
Feel their souls in pity move,
This will ease the burd'ning grief,
This to sorrows give relief!

Parents sad—this tribute take,
And your hearts to joy awake!
Think—tho' of your babes bereft,
They a world of sin have left;
Safe, behind yon starry sky—
Lo! they live—no more can die!

Parents blest—O weep no more,
Sadness, sorrow, all be o'er!
Children, whom you dearly loved,
God has kindly hence removed!
Sin and death for them are o'er,
Parents blest—O weep no more!

Scenes of bliss successive rise—
Mansions—lo! in Paradise!
Children whom you dearly loved,
God has to yon world removed;
Safe now home—their dangers o'er,
Parents blest—then weep no more!

PANCHARIS—A PARAPHRASE.

Christian, know thy high vocation,
Lo! by grace a child of God!
Glad, sustain this dear relation,
Purchase of redeeming blood;
Sinner once—with sinners straying,
Lost and wretched, doomed to death,
Sinner now—with saints obeying,
Sharer of "like precious faith."

Rescued from thy sad condition,
Sin, defilement, guilt and shame—
From estrangement, base ambition,
Safe—redeemed in Jesus' name—

Friend esteemed, an heir of heaven,
  " Righteous" made in Him that died,
Free—all blessings thee be given—
  " Grace and Peace be multiplied."

"All things," here to life pertaining,
  Needful to salvation deemed,
In the Saviour's blood obtaining,
  By His death from death redeemed—
"All things" are His loved ones given,
  Purchased—saved by grace divine—
Called to virtue, bliss, and heaven,
  Christian, thus, are all things thine!

Promised gifts all thought transcending,
  " Precious and exceeding great"—
Blessings, Pilgrim, thee attending,
  Rescued from thy lost estate—
Sin, pollution, guilt, escaping,
  Sharing now a life divine—
Strength to stand, each snare evading,
  Christian, lo! this grace is thine!

Free from every false relation—
  Free from sin, and guilt, and death,
Earnest, heed thy high vocation,
  Serious, guard thy " precious faith,"
Watchful still in each connection,
  To thy faith be " virtue " joined—
Firm to give each grace protection,
  Kindly thus of God designed!

These now had in full possession,
  Guards to every danger nigh—
Still enhancing thy profession,
  " Knowledge" add to gifts so high;

And to knowledge, keen-eyed mistress,
  " Temp'rance " forms a fitting maid,
Join yet " Patience "—gentle victress—
  All thy hopes on her be stayed!

And to Patience—suff'ring meekness,
  " Godliness " be closely joined—
Adding still a creature " Kindness "
  Comfort for the poor designed—
And to crown these all with beauty,
  Precious, brightest, purest gem—
Life and soul of christian duty,
  " Charity" be joined with them!

For, these things in due relation,
  If in thee, and there abound—
They shall make thee in thy station,
  " Sterile" not, nor " fruitless" found;
He, who lacks these central graces,
  Sure is blind, and cannot see—
He forgets his deep-stained vices,
  Purged from which, he now is free!

Wherefore, strive more bravely, Christian,
  Careful, make thy calling sure—
If once clear be thine election,
  Thou shalt ever stand secure;
For an " Entrance" to yon mansion,
  Kingdom of thy gracious Lord—
Thine beyond the blue expansion,
  Christian, is thy " great reward!"

WELCOME TO " X. Y. Z." THE SECOND.

At times we smile, and sometimes weep,
As o'er the weekly sheet we peep;

The various "news" a glance secure,
And some repel, and some allure.
To-day I smiled, and smile as yet,
To see—a second "X—Y—Z."

'Tis pleasant, surely, now and then,
To see one's "name" in print again,
Since on this hangs the writer's fame,
That virtuous men repeat his name,
Then hail my pen, without regret,
As friend—this second "X—Y—Z."

Our bus'ness we, may each attend,
Nor less of "composition" send—
There's work enough for each to do—
There's work enough for me and you.
Then hands we join, without regret,
The first and second—"X—Y—Z."

DON'T ABUSE THIS SPORTIVE DAY.

FOURTH OF JULY SONG.

Teachers.

Little children, brisk and gay,
Don't abuse this sportive day!
  Cheerful, lively, full of glee,
  We are pleased each one to see;
Children, only, we would say,
Don't abuse this sportive day!

Children.

Kindest teachers, fond and dear,
Merry here we all appear!
  Cheerful is the day begun,

Oh ! we'll have a heap of fun ;
Teachers, then, we children gay
Won't abuse this sportive day !

Teachers.

Children high and children low,
Welcome here, and cheerful go !
Pleasant, merry, all may be,
Full of fun and full of glee ;
Only, children, we would say
Don't abuse this sportive day !

Children.

Teachers young and teachers old,
Here we come a curious fold,
    Some are little—older some,
    But we all together come,
Singing, we, so glad and gay,
Won't abuse this sportive day !

Teachers and Children.

Teachers grave, and children gay,
All seem young and brisk to-day ;
    Strange it is—but so it goes,
    How it is, one hardly knows ;
Teachers grave, and children gay,
Won't abuse this sportive day !

Omnes.

Joining all we cheerful raise
To our God a song of praise ;
    He sustains both great and small,
    Children, Teachers, friends and all,
Cheerful, then, we jointly say,
Don't abuse this sportive day !

ACROSTIC.

Gone, Dear Brother, to realms of love,
Eternal life to taste above—
Oh ! how divine, how sweet thy rest,
Reclining on the Saviour's breast !
Glorious thought—reflection sweet,
Etherial songs thy joys repeat !
JEHOVAH, Lord of earth and heav'n,
Hath to thee rest eternal giv'n.
Enjoy that rest—that sacred rest,
In sweet communion with the blest ;
Secure from pain, from danger free,
Long shall thy blissful portion be,
Eternal life—without alloy—
Replete with songs of sacred joy !

REFLECTIONS.

Hark ! Hark ! a lovely voice descends,
Look up, ye now surviving friends,
Come, parents, brothers, sisters, come,
Accept this sweet, this sacred home.

Behold ! in yonder spheres sublime,
There reigns your Saviour all Divine ;
'Tis He, who once for sinners died,
Now pleads your cause in mercy's sight.

Oh ! will you, can you yet delay,
And not the Saviour's voice obey ?
How can you still His love deride,
Who, on the cross, to save you died ?

Oh! can you, notwithstanding all
The strong appeals of mercy's call,
The Saviour of mankind despise,
And risk your title to the skies?

Oh! will you live from day to day,
And with the foolish worldling say,
My soul, now take thy wonted ease,
Thy goods, laid up, will never cease!

Oh! will you spend your life in vain,
And have your souls in sin remain?
Say—will you live without a thought
Of death, of judgment, and of God?

If this you do, there is a place,
Where pain and sorrow never cease;
And in that place their home must be,
Who slight His love, so vast, so free!

But should you now to Jesus come,
On high will be your lasting home;
And there may you for ever sing
The praises of your heav'nly king!

Come, then, and all with one accord,
Accept the offers of your Lord;
Come, make His grace your all in all,
And you shall never, never, fall.

Thus speaks the mercy of the Lord
In sweetest language of His word:
"Return, O wanderers, return
And I will love you as mine own.'

Oh! may this light of Love divine
Upon your souls in mercy shine;

Conduct you in that pleasant way
Which issues in an endless day !

O state, beyond conception sweet,
With joys divine and love replete ;
A life—in which unceasing roll
Oceans of bliss across the soul !

Oh ! will you not for such a day,
To Christ your loving Saviour pray ?
A day—whose sunny beams how bright,
Th' eternal God himself the light !

Then come, obey your Saviour's voice,
And make the Lord your early choice !
So shall you dwell with Him above,
And feast upon redeeming love !

Hark ! Hark ! the Saviour calls once more
Ere yet your day of grace is o'er—
Oh ! heed this sweet, this loving call,
And freely choose Him one and all !

THE PRODIGAL SON.

In figures the Saviour of men was rehearsing
  The madness and folly which oft He had seen,
When, lo ! in review, the thick darkness dispersing,
  A picture stood forth as in life it had been ;
This purpose for, wisely, a " certain man" choosing,
  To whom in much mercy " two sons" had been given,
He sketched the sad issues of freedom abusing,
  A picture like Hades in contrast with heaven.

The younger, his portion of substance requesting,
  Cried : " Give me, my Father, the goods that are due ;
Though sorry the peace of my Parent molesting,
  I'm going—I cannot stay longer with you ;"
In anguish of spirit the Father was musing
  O'er scenes the lone stranger would likeliest meet,
Yet, found he could stay not the tender boy losing,
  And kindly the portion laid down at his feet !

The youth so impatient, " not many days" pausing,
  His treasures collected, safe, firmly secured,
Away and away went the youngster rejoicing,
  Far, far from his homestead by fancies allured ;
Absolved from his bondage, and virtue discarding,
  In wickedness soon the dear youth became rife,
And, not the good counsels of Parent regarding,
  " There wasted his substance in riotous life."

And when, so profusely his resources wasting,
  He noticed, at last, that his treasures were gone,
Quick on to his ruin by famine still hasting,
  He found to his sorrow himself was undone ;
Thus forced to employment so sadly degrading,
  The means of subsistence most coldly denied,
He fain would—his highly-wrought fancies abating,
  Have been with the " swine" in his living allied.

Oh ! sad to the youth in such fancies abounding,
  This state must have proved in his awful extreme,
As e'en the rude " husks," tho' his pathway surrounding,
  Denied him, as means of subsistence, had been ;
Wo, wo to transgressors !—All reason dethroning,
  Sin leaves the poor wretch a sad victim of shame ;
And prostrate in dust—his sad bondage bemoaning,
  He feels on him rests the whole burden of blame.

And here, now, to home-life his fancies recurring,
  He calls to remembrance the scenes of his youth,
And glad to his freedom those pleasures preferring,
  Enjoyments connected with virtue and truth—
" He came to himself," and—most humbly confessing
  His sins—he exclaimed, with a spirit illumed,
" Our servants have bread, in abundance possessing,
  Whilst here I, poor wretch, am with hunger consumed."

Aroused by his sorrows—his conscience oppressing,
  He formed the good purpose : " I now will arise,
And go to my Father—my failures confessing—
  Say, Father, I've sinned against Thee and the skies,
I am no more worthy—thy mandates transgressing,
  A son to be called, or thy grace to receive ;
Still, Father, forgive me, O richest in blessing,
  Thy servant but make me, my sorrows relieve ?"

By grace thus assisted—these tho'ts still revolving,
  To come to his Father, he quickly arose—
His Father there saw him,—on mercy resolving,
  He hastened with pleasure his love to propose ;
And kindly fell on him, his dear one embracing,
  And " kissed" the sweet boy with a father's strong love;
" My mercies are boundless, thy sins all effacing,
  I will be thy Father—thy home be above."

The soul-stricken sinner, his wand'rings bewailing,
  Confessed himself worthless, polluted, and vile ;
The father still loved him, his mercies prevailing,
  He met him in kindness—his fear with a smile :
" Go, hasten to clothe him, the richest robe bringing,
  His hand on, a ringlet, and shoes on his feet—
Let's eat and be merry, all cheerfully singing,
  My son that is found, let us joyfully greet."

MARTYR HYMN OF THE EARLY CHURCH.

FROM THE LATIN.

Th' eternal gifts of Christ, the King,
And victories of martyrs strong,
Their well-deserved praise we sing
With souls elate and cheerful song!

The Princes of Thy church were they,
Triumphant leaders of the fight,
Brave soldiers of celestial ray—
The erring world's substantial light!

The terrors of this life endured,
And pains of body all despised,
By hope of sacred death allured,
A blissful life they realized!

The martyrs to the flames consigned,
To teeth of cruel beasts of prey—
With instruments of torture armed,
The hand of malice seeks to slay!

Denuded though their viscera—
Their sacred blood effused in strife,
Still calm and undisturbed are they,
By strength of a perennial life!

Firm is Thy saints' devoted faith,
And undismayed Thy people's trust;
The precious, priceless, grace of Christ
Still triumphs o'er the sons of dust!

In them the Father's glory shines,
  In them the Son's good-will we meet,
In them exults the Spirit blest,
  And Heaven with rapture is replete!

Thee now, Reedemer, we beseech,
  That, with their blissful host above,
Thou wouldst Thy praying saints unite
  In an eternal bond of love!

GRABSCHRIFT.

Rosen! warum blueht ihr hier
  Frœlich auf dem kuehlen Grabe?
Pilgrim! dass wir geben dir
  Hoffnung—schœnste Himmels-Gabe!

Rosen! und, nach kurzem Lauf,
  Doch verblueht was hier zu sehen?
Pilgrim! es blueht wieder auf
  In den schoœnen Himmels-hœhen!

HYMN OF ST. CLEMENT.

FROM THE GREEK.

Thou Rector of indocile youth,
Thou Pinion of unerring birds,
Of infants small the safest Guide,
And Shepherd of Thy royal Lambs,
Thy simple children congregate
      To sacred praise,
      Sincere, to sing
      With guileless lips

The Leader of Thy children—Christ !
Thou King of saints,
All-swaying Word
The Holy Father of—Most High !
Of wisdom Chief,
The lab'rer's Stay,
Unfailing Joy—
Of human kind
The strong Deliv rer, Jesus, Thou !
Shepherd, Vintner,
Guide—Director,
Wing Supernal
Of Thy most holy—blessed flock !
Angler of men—
The rescued, saved
From ocean vile—
The stainless fish
From hostile waves
Alluring—to delicious Life !
Guide—of human
Sheep the Pastor,
Sacred Leader,
O King of inexperienced youth !
Foot-steps of Christ,
Celestial Way,
Unfailing Word,
Perennial Age,
Eternal Light,
Sweet mercy's Font,
And virtue's Soul,
Sweet Life of those
Loud praising God—O Jesus Christ !
Celestial Milk
Of sweetest breasts,
The grace-dispensing Bride's rich boon,

The Essence of Thy wisdom pure !
    Thy Children dear
    Of guileless lips
    Have nourished been
    Of Reason's breast,
With spirit chaste completely filled !
    Praise simple, then,
    And Hymns sincere,
Ascending, hail our King—the Christ !
    The sacred gifts
    Of living lore—
    We jointly sing,
    Sincerely sing
The valiant Son—blest Prince of grace !
    Chorus of Peace,
    In Christ renewed,
    Sweet Wisdom's race,
Let's jointly sing—the God of Peace !

HEAVEN.

There is a place than all more sweet,
With sacred joy—with bliss replete,
Where virtues all most sweetly blend,
Where friend communion holds with friend.

'Tis found where saints in rapture meet,
Where spirits pure such spirits greet—
'Tis found where Christ supremely reigns,
And angels chant their lofty strains.

And in that world, and on that spot,
The brilliant prospect changeth not,
Each day brings on a lovlier view,
And joy succeeds each joy anew !

Sweet, sacred spot! There softly rest,
My ransomed soul 'mid spirits blest!
And when Life's short career doth close,
Then grant me but in thee repose!

THE MARYS AT THE SAVIOUR'S TOMB.

'Twas when the day began to dawn,
  To see His tomb the Marys came,
By strong affection thither drawn,
  For Tear-drop is their common name.

An Angel rolled the rock away,
  And, musing, still sat on the stone,
His " raiment" white—of purest ray,
  His countenance most brilliant shone.

He saw the fairy creatures come,
  And, smiling, " fear not" seemed to say ;
The Saviour's risen, 'live and gone,
  Come see the " place" where Jesus lay!

Go—quickly His disciples tell
  The Master's risen from the dead,
And, where the Galileans dwell,
  Lo! ye shall see Him as He said !

And they, departing quickly thence,
  Made haste to tell the wond'rous tale ;
While on their way, in deep suspense,
  There met them Jesus, saying—" hail !"

" All hail"—how strange, so charming, sweet,
  They knew Him, 'twas His gracious word,
And, prostrate at the Saviour's feet,
  They worship now their risen Lord !

And, gazing on the trembling fair—
" Be not afraid" the Saviour said,
"Go, tell.my brethren, they shall there,
In Galilee, see Me, their Head !"

O sacred place! O moment blest,
That saw the Lord alive again!
His triumphs are to sinners rest,
His risen life—the life of men !

The Marys on this word relied—
The joyful news were quickly spread,
He's here again—the crucified—
" The Saviour's risen from the dead !"

The trembling saints cheer up again,
Anew their dying hopes revive,
Their murdered Lord is back with them,
Sure pledge of an immortal life !

GRABSCHRIFT.

Traurend steht ihr an dem Grabe,
Finster scheint der Todten Haus ;
Doch, ich schœne Hoffnung habe,
Einstens komm ich froh heraus ;
Den ihr liebtet hier bei Leben,
Wird euch Gott dort wieder geben !

DARE TO BE TRUE.

In what you do, or think, or write,
Let wisdom all thy tho'ts indite,
And act the paltry wits despite !

ALBUM—"WHITE."

An "Album" seems a curious thing,
A "subject" not—not quite a "king,"
'Tis honored by a num'rous train,
Yet, looks on none with proud disdain.
'Tis Album called—in English "white,"
Tho' in it "Scribs" presume to write.

But why a thing, both "white" and "black,"
In NAME should either feature lack,
You can't with any grace demand
That I at all should understand.
The sky is "gloomy" called, you know,
Sometimes, alas! in time of snow—
Then, why, tho' common sense despite,
May we not call it "Album"—white?

If I should, now, this thing define
According to these views of mine,
I could not better do, methinks,
Than call it an Egyptian "Sphinx."
This course, tho' each most clearly saw,
Were not according quite to "law"—
Yet, since I have no better name,
Will any my misfortune blame?

This "Album," then, a nameless thing,
A "subject" not—nor quite a "king,"
We have presumed—with praise or blame?
An Eastern, mystic "Sphinx" to name.

But since this "Album" can't be quite
An Album pure—a spotless "white,"
May gentlemen, with stain or blot,
Or impure lines—disgrace it not!

And ladies—may I venture here,
To check a too excessive cheer?—
Ye ladies, most supremely chaste,
Be modest—shun a vicious taste!
Where vice supreme dominion gains,
No beauty, pathos, charm remains;
Sometimes, in one unguarded line,
Fair virtue sinks—bright gem divine!
Avoid this rock, in Life's dark main,
On which who founders sinks in shame.
Sad wreck!—A charmless form alone,
A spectre's left—the Lady's gone!!

THE PILGRIMS' SONG.

FROM THE GERMAN.

The following beautiful song is attached to a German edition of the "IMITATIO CHRISTI," by Thomas a Kempis, and is designed as an encouragement to weary pilgrims on their way to the "land of the blest." The translation is literal throughout, and faithful to the original, so far as the nature of the subject, and the peculiarity of the metre would admit.

Come, children, let us journey,
    The ev'ning shades make haste;
'Tis dangerous here to linger,
    Within this barren waste;
    Come, be your strength renew'd,
To endless life advancing,
Your graces still enhancing,
    The end's supremely good!

We shall not view regretful,
The narrow pilgrim-path,
We know full-well the Faithful,
Who us invited hath ;
Come follow, then, and trust Him,
With strong affection burning,
Each one his visage turning,
Straight to Jerusalem !

The parting—thus effected—
Cannot but pleasant be,
Things better are expected
When quite released and free ;
Then, children, fear not—no !
A thousand worlds despising,
Their threat'ning and enticing,
Still on your journey go !

When nature firm opposing,
Your course is good and fair ;
While flesh and sense some choosing,
Most wretched pilgrims are ;
Then leave the creature—leave
Whate'er of sin partaking,
And, e'en yourselves forsaking,
The mighty work achieve !

Like pilgrims we must journey,
Free—truly nude and poor,
Much gath'ring, keeping, lugging,
Our falt'ring steps allure ;
Who likes, his death may speed ;
WE journey quite denuded—
With little wealth included,
That serves in time of need !

Supreme, your hearts adorning,
    Nor body else nor dome;
We're strangers here sojourning,
    Must soon forsake our home;
Concern brings bitter grief—
A pilgrim. well preparing,
Endureth, though despairing,
    The pilgrimage so brief!

Nor let us much be viewing
    The trinkets by the way;
Thus halting—these pursuing,
    Occasions much delay;
    These follies—all be gone!
Thro' thick and thin proceeding,
Nor trifling senses heeding,
    The vict'ry soon is won!

E'en though the way be narrow,
    Quite rugged, lone, and steep,
With thorny weeds abounding,
    With many a cross—and deep!
    'Tis still but Nature's way;
Enough!—yet still proceeding,
Our blessed Leader heeding,
    We break through ev'ry stay!

What hearing here and seeing,
    We scarcely hear and see;
We leave it, then, still fleeing,
    No dream shall heeded be;
    We crave——eternity;
With God communion seekng,
Our walk in Heaven's keeping,
    Our souls and all shall be!

We journey on unnoticed,
 Despised and unknown;
And scarcely seen or heeded,
 Or heard so far from home:
 And when we heeded are,
We're heard and heeded singing
The joys which time is bringing,
 In yonder regions fair!

Come, children, let us journey,
 The Father goes along.
Our feeble steps supporting
 In tempest fierce and strong;
 And courage He will give,
With sweetest beams alluring,
Still calling and assuring;
 Oh! blissful, thus to live!

Let each one, cheerful hast'ning,
 Pursue the great reward;
The fiery "cloud" regarding,
 The presence of the Lord;
 The eye but linger may,
Where beck'ning Love, enticing
Him, thus, not her despising,
 Conducts in wisdom's way!

The Lamb's sweet image bearing,
 'Twill be on us impressed,
And in our walk appearing,
 So childlike—so depressed!
 So gentle, mild, and meek,
The lambkins, onward straying,
Their shepherd's voice obeying,
 His will alone they seek!

Come, children, let's be moving,
    We're going hand in hand ;
Each one with each conjoining,
    In this wild desert land ;
    Come, let us childlike be,
Not by the way contending,
While angel-bands attending,
    As brethren frank and free !

Should e'er some weak one falter,
    ·Ye strong ones bear him on ;
Thus each the other aiding,
    Let peace and love be shown ;
    Come, be ye closely bound ;
The lowest rank each taking,
And every sin forsaking,
    Here on this sacred ground !

Come, cheerful let's be going,
    Still short'ning is our road ;
Each day this comfort knowing,
    We'll soon reach our abode ;
    Some little courage more !
To each be Jesus nearer,
His grace than all things dearer,
    We'll, thus, reach Heaven's shore !

Not longer much enduring
    The time for us to roam—
Not longer much enduring,
    And we shall be at home ;
    There shall we be at rest,
When we with all the pious,
Shall to our Father hie us,
    O, how supremely blest !

On this dear truth relying,
  'Tis well our risking worth—
And wholly that denying
  Which chains us down to earth,
  The world is far too small ;
Thro' Jesus, dead and bleeding,
To endless life succeeding—
  Be Christ our "ALL IN ALL !"

O friend, in whom believing,
  Thou all attracting POLE,
Thou ever-blest Redeemer,
  How charmest Thou the soul !
  We all rejoice in Thee—
Our Joy and Life enduring,
Each blessing still procuring,
  Our only comfort be !

HAPPY IN GOD'S LOVE.

FROM THE GERMAN.

I now have found that firm foundation,
  Which ever holds my anchor sure ;
Where else but in the wounds of Jesus,
  Where ere the world it lay secure—
The Rock, which stands unmoved and firm,
When Heaven and Earth to chaos turn !

It is that changeless, deep, compassion,
  Which far all human thought transcends ;
It is the love-fraught arms' extension
  Of Him who to the sinner bends—
Whose heart doth o'er us wretches break,
That we may not to Judgment 'wake !

We are not, hopeless, doomed to perish,
  God wills that we should help obtain ;
'Twas hence the Son, on earth appearing,
  To heaven, at length, returned again—
'Tis hence He knocks—knocks evermore
So urgent at our hard heart's door !

O Well-spring ! which, our sins o'erwhelming,
  Hath vanquished them thro' Jesus' death ;
'Tis, thus, our wounds are healed securely,
  Here, now, is no condemning breath ;
Since Jesus' bloodiest Sacrifice,
Compassion, Lord ! unceasing cries !

Therein, believing, will I hide me,
  To Him my trembling soul confide ;
And, when my num'rous sins afflict me,
  Anon, I'll hasten to His side—
There is, till Time's last note shall sound,
Compassion sweet, unceasing, found !

Though ev'rything from me be wrested,
  Which body can or soul revive—
Though I no comfort here may cherish,
  And stript may seem of all but life—
Though distant far deliv'rance be,
Yet still compassion's left for me !

Should e'er this mortal life oppress me,
  Aud sorrows rise and sore distress,
That I—by many a care distracted—
  My foolish thoughts must yet confess ;
And should I hence be sorely tried,
Still—in compassion I'll confide !

Must I, in all my best endeavors,
　Whereby to serve my God I've sought,
Much imperfection still discover,
　My boasting then, indeed, is naught;
Yet shall this comfort still remain,
Compassion gives me hope again !

May things but go His will according,
　With whom so much compassion is,
May He Himself my heart replenish
　With grace, that it forget not this :
Thus standeth it, in love and pain,
While His compassion doth remain !

On this firm ground will I continue
　So long as Earth shall bear my feet;
Thus will I think—thus do, and practice
　Until my heart shall cease to beat—
Then will I sing, with bliss elate,
O Well-spring of compassion great !

JESUS—THE SOURCE OF BLISS.

FROM THE GERMAN.

The following is a version of one of the most touching of German Hymns. The translation is, upon the whole, a literal one. The ninth and tenth stanzas, however, it has been found necessary to change somewhat, and to extend them to five stanzas, in order fully to bring out the sense of the original. In all other respects, I have attempted to preserve both the form and spirit of the German original.

Jesus, lo, my soul's sweet rest,
　And of Treasures far the best !
"All in all" art Thou to me,
　And forever "all" shalt be !

Are there those, to whom are dear
Treasures, gold, possessions here ;
Jesus, and His precious blood
Are to me than all more good !

When my foes in fierce array,
Openly obstruct my way ;
Jesus every fear doth quell,
Conquers Satan, sin, and hell !

Am I sick—and none is near,
Who my fainting soul can cheer ;
Jesus—my physician—will
Be in death my comfort still !

Am I wretched—steeped in care,
Of provision stript and bare ;
Jesus timely aid affords,
And my sinking frame supports !

Must I with a drooping heart,
Friends forsake—my home depart ;
Jesus my distress doth share,
Strangely still protects me there !

Must I scorn endure and shame,
Cast on God—and on his name ;
Jesus gives me secret might,
And his " shame" is my delight !

If in honey—strength and glee,
And in sugar—sweetness be ;
Jesus—richest source of bliss,
Precious more, and sweeter is !

Sounds seraphic charm mine ear,
Sweetest music oft I hear ;

Jesus—name divinely sweet,
Only can the charm complete!

Pleasing objects meet mine eye,
Scene sublime with scene doth vie;
Jesus—Sharon's Rose divine,
Doth each radiant charm combine!

Richest, rarest viands, here,
Sweetest fruits my palate cheer;
Jesus—mystic " bread of life,"
Doth my sinking soul revive!

Frequent I my hand extend,
Cheerful to embrace a friend;
Jesus—friend of all the best,
Makes alone supremely blest!

Jesus—meat divine and drink,
Spice of all I know or think;
Jesus—richest theme for praise,
Sing my soul thro' endless days!

Jesus—source of BLISS to me,
Let me share a part in THEE!
By Thy passion—by Thy blood,
Reconcile my soul to God!

And in death—supremely good—
Jesus! may Thy precious' blood,
May Thy groans, Thy dying breath,
Be my strength—my Life in death!

THY PEOPLE GREET.

Jesus, with assurance sweet,
Graciously Thy people greet,
When to worship Thee they meet,
    At Thy feet!

FROM FORTY-NINE TO FIFTY.

Hail! Patrons, hail! each precious gift divine—life,
    health, each joy,
These, on this New-year's morn, are wishes from your
    "Carrier boy!"

The old year's sudden death—the new year's birth I sing,
And still the weekly "News," select, delicious bring—
Through summer's sun, thro' winter's storm and dashing
    rains I came,
When heat oppressed—when piercing winds did rack my
    tender frame,
For all this toil, exposed to summer's burning sun,
    To winter's snowy drift—
For all this toil, your Carrier, patrons, justly claims
    From you a New-year's gift!

We once could justly boast of 4 T 9,
But Tempus now has stepp'd A † the ——
The B Z year, 2 B Z, closed his I's,
B 4 a new year's **O** had time to rise.
Of naught on earth R U allowed 2 say
It brings no †, M ⌣ ⌣ no D K;
Y, don't U C, stern fate B 4 U stands
And waits 2 lay on U its I C ☞ ☞ ?
'Tis M T trash, 2 speak of bliss below
When * * grow dim and Life's N M T show,
This ‖ looks quite 2 odd, U C,
As coffee does when U R asked 2 T.
But, Y, U ask, the **O** and * * M ⌣ ?
A few more —— ——, 2 answer U, I'll trace :

'Tis but 2 show that fools can cut a ——
And E Z write some — — of M T trash,
But N E Wit, 2 kindle pure delight,
B 4 he writes, should first M ⁓⁓ the light.

———

Wake up, my muse—in sweet and mellow verse,
Such scenes as mark the present age rehearse ;
Each age has some peculiar phase or side,
Which serves the skilful artisan as guide ;
May Wisdom's steady hand my pen direct
To draw the deeds of men, and facts, correct ;
And Thou, the source of every gift divine,
Vouchsafe this grace—that I be wholly thine !

The rocking main—the rushing tide of life,
Unstayed by sin—by war, or bloody strife,
By falsehood. cunning schemes, or low device,
By noblest deeds, or tyrants' fall and rise—
This rushing tide—this rolling sea sublime
From off God's book, the mystic scroll of time
Has rolled, unfolded—is unfolding still
In radiant lines, in gloom, JEHOVAH's will.

What Moses in the Law—what Prophets spake,
Apostles preached or Martyrs at the stake,
Each grand event and every act minute,
From petty squabble up to fierce dispute,
All public woes, and tears in private shed
By children, youths, and men of hoary head,
The gath'ring storms, distress, and sweet repose,
In TIME's great book, the checkered page compose !

What stirring scenes with each revolving year
On Life's broad bosom witnessed, disappear,
Unknown, mysterious scenes of light and gloom,
Yet each has limits fixed—a certain doom ;

Thus, on Life's troubled sea, storm-tossed and dark,
Unerring Wisdom guides our fragile bark;
JEHOVAH reigns, and "makes the wrath of man"
To praise Him—and unfold His wondrous plan.

The mystic "time and times and half a time,"
Big with the fates of men—with truths sublime,
From age to age—the beacon light has stood
To warn the wicked, and to cheer the good ;
The facts—educed by each successive year,
Have added light and made the sense more clear,
Till now,.in these our own eventful days,
The WORD its brilliant light, in fact, displays.

Time's rugged car, entrenched in fiery wheels,
Moves on ; the earth, 'neath vengeance stagg'ring, reels ;
On every side the sound of war is heard,
And wrath divine and judgments long deferred ;
The nations quake—the troubled sea doth roar,
And kingdoms fall, and tyrants reign no more ;
These scenes in one bright flood of light combine
To illustrate, and prove God's book DIVINE !

Lo ! in what strange confusion Earth appears,
Some by ambition bound—some mad with fears ;
Too long had brutal passions, unrestrained,
Their course pursued—the world of comfort drained,
Till from the wretched, cries for help arose
To Him, who doth on earth each lot dispose ;
Their piteous cry was heard, and from the Lord
Avenging justice came—the fiery sword !

Imperial Rome from 'neath the gath'ring gloom,
Astonished, heard her long appointed doom ;
Her throne, baptised in seas of human gore,
From off its base was hurled to rise no more.

On wings of light the startling news were spread,
And joy filled many a heart, and some a dread !
Europa's chains, no more the mass appall,
From off devoted necks the shackles fall !

But see, the vulgar crowd, released from chains,
Within no proper bounds the mass remains ;
For as the mountain torrents wildly bound
Down dizzy steeps, and waste the country round,
So the fierce passions, raging uncontrolled,
In wasting torrents o'er the country rolled,
Till from on high, armed with resistless will
JEVOHAH spake His mighty : " Peace, be still !"

Mysterious year—this year of "forty-nine,"
What brilliant deeds, what cruel wars are thine !
What multitudes of friends and home deprived,
And numbers more in glory safe arrived,
Many a child of parents both bereft,
And widows poor to mourn their loss are left ;
For these—when stript of every joy beside,
Do Thou, O God, in tender love provide !

But, lo ! amid these various scenes of strife,
Triumphant reigns the blessed " Prince of Life,"
Depending on His arm, and near His side.
Moves like a radiant cloud the Church, His " bride ;"
Redeemed from sin, His faithful band will know
No bliss, but in His smile, while here below,
And longing wait, in yonder sphere sublime,
To sing His endless praise, thro' endless time !

How beauteous are their feet, who peace proclaim,
And offer life and bliss in Jesus' name ;
" Their paths are paths of peace"—at home, abroad,
They prospering see the gracious work of God !

Around spring temples up, and from them rise
Bright clouds of fragrant incense to the skies—
And God, to whom are due all love and praise,
Doth on His churches shed rich gifts of grace!

Such are the objects, such the work sublime,
Which here do occupy the Christian's time.
Blest work! in which my Saviour took a part,
To publish peace—to heal the broken heart!
For this my weekly messages are brought
With truth divine, with every virtue fraught;
Without display I pass from door to door
To please the rich and cheer the humble poor.

This time, as ever, has my New-year's song
Grown line by line until it's much too long;
But blame me not—the song's at your control,
Unless you choose, you need not read the whole ;
For well I know, that what's UNWILLING read,
Like silly dreams, can but disturb the head.
I'll drop the thing—submit the whole to you,
And, parting, say to each, to all—ADIEU!

FOR AN ALBUM.

The following six lines, signed E. W. R., were written by the Rev. E.
W. Reinecke, D. D., on the blue leaf of an Album. On the opposite
leaf was an anchor drawn, and in connection with it, the Scripture
words: "Hope is the anchor of the Soul." Immediately below it
were written the last eight lines signed D. Y. H.

"HOPE IS THE ANCHOR OF THE SOUL."

But when Time's billows wildly roll ;
When thy frail bark is rudely tost
By tempest high , and all seems lost ;
Where is the rock on which to cast
This anchor holding sure and fast?
    "The Rock of Ages."   E W. R.

" E. William R.," and " D.—Y.—H.,"
Of habits like, and like in age—
Two sportive friends, both firm and true,
Conjointly use this page of " blue,"
Prophetic—as the story goes—
Of future bliss, of banished woes,
Fit EMBLEM, as a friendly scroll,
Of Hope—" the anchor of the soul."

I WISH HER DREAM WERE TRUE!

A lady friend dreamt that she was in a sick room where the GUAR-
DIAN was found. Presently the attending physician came in, and,
casting his eyes around, fixed them intently upon the table on which
some copies of the GUARDIAN were lying, when, with great vehe-
mence, he exclaimed : "My God, what can this mean? The GUARDIAN
in every house I come to!"

I wish her Dream were true—
That in each cot and palace round,
Were truly thus " THE GUARDIAN" found,
Ceaseless, in strains of sweetest sound,
    To breathe its tales of love !

I wish her Dream were true—
That, gathered round the social hearth,
In serious mood or playful mirth,
The young—the brightest hopes of earth,
    The Guardian all might read !

I wish her Dream were true—
That, when this treach'rous sea of life,
Arrayed in smiles, or fierce with strife,
Allures to scenes with mischief rife,
    The Guardian then were near !

I wish her Dream were true—
That, in this dreary world below,
Where sadly roam the high—the low,
A refuge, when the rough winds blow,
   The Guardian might afford !

I wish her Dream were true—
That, when the pilgrim sore is prest,
Care-worn and sad—by sin distrest,
And grief sits nestling in the breast,
   The Guardian then might cheer !

I wish her dream were true—
That when disease in open day
Nor nightly doth its progress stay,
Aud every earthly joy gives way,
   The Guardian's voice were near !

I wish her dream were true—
That, where physicians e'er are seen,
Were heard : " My God, what can this mean,
In every house and cot, I ween,
   The Guardian I must meet !"

MODEL WOMEN.

With permission kindly given,
Founded on decrees of heaven,
Here a picture I submit—
Sketch approved in Holy Writ :
Where, as in a glass, are seen
WIVES divinely fair, I ween ;
Women God doth well approve,
Women mortals fain would love !

Chaste in conversation they,
Fear their husbands and obey;
Whose adorning sure will not
Outward be, and soon forgot;
Not apparel, rich and fair,
Wear of gold or plait of hair.

GENTLENESS beseemeth them
Better far than gold or gem;
Ornament divinely fair,
Time doth not its worth impair;
Exquisite—to grace the end,
Love and meekness sweetly blend:
GEMS—tho' many prize them not,
Precious in the sight of God!

CHRIST APPEARING TO THE TWO MARYS.

Scarcely had the shades of night
  Yielded to the dawn of day,
Ere the Marys came in sight
  Where the sleeping Saviour lay.

Scenes of danger heeding not,
  At the grave they both appear,
Anxious o'er the sacred spot
  Each to shed affection's tear.

Suddenly a vision bright
  Stands before their ravished eyes:
Gazing on the lovely sight,
  They do hear with sweet surprise:

" Fear not, for I know ye seek
  Jesus, which was crucified,

He is risen—once the weak—
See the place He occupied.

" Quickly go—the story tell,
He is risen from the dead ;
Vanquished now the gates of hell,
Death itself is captive led !

" Haste ye, lo ! the Lord has gone,
Yonder in sweet Galilee,
Where His mighty works were done,
There shall ye the Saviour see !"

Quickly thence departing, they—
Glad, to see their risen Lord,
And the heav'nly voice obey—
Bring to His disciples word.

Cheerily they speed their " way"
Fair as Eden's shady bow'rs
Blest, in blessing others, they—
Lo ! their path is decked with flow'rs !

On their pleasing errand gone,
Jesus meets them, saying : " Hail !"
Touching scene ! to sketch alone
Pen alike and pencil fail !

Lowly bending at His feet,
They their risen Lord adore ;
Jesus kindly doth repeat,
What the Angel spake before :

" Go—my weeping brethren tell
That they haste to Galilee—
There, triumphant over hell,
Me, their Saviour they shall see !"

O ! it was a precious time,
  Gracious were the words He spake ;
Jesus seen—His form divine
  Did in them each joy awake !

CANTIQUE DU VETERAN.

FROM THE FRENCH.

How long, how long, with fears distrest,
  Wilt Thou, thus LOW, behold me bro't ?
How long, how long, with guilt opprest,
  Must I see me by THEE forgot ?
O, why for ever, God severe—
  Away from me Thine eye dost turn ?
Ah ! art Thou not a Father dear—
  The sweetest HOPE of them that mourn ?

By night—by day—I Thee implore,
  Appease my troubled heart in me !
Speak peace, O God, my soul unto,
  O Lord, no longer angry be !
O, deign my wretched heart to cheer,
  On me a gracious eye to turn !
Oh ! Thou art e'er a Father dear—
  The sweetest HOPE of them that mourn !

Now near the tomb—my body cold—
  Death seizes on my senses sure ;
O Lord, Thy pard'ning grace unfold
  Unto an "old man" sad and poor !
My soul doth hope in Christ, so near,
  With HIM may I in heaven sojourn ;
O Lord, Thou art a Father dear—
  The sweetest HOPE of them that mourn !

Blest he, that in the Lord doth die,
His soul redeemed the Saviour by ;
  He sweetly rests from all his pains—
From all his sorrows he released,
From all his woes and labours eased,
  From all his foes and from his chains ;
To Heaven his works do him succeed,
When Christ will make him blest indeed !

IMPROMPTU ON WRITING A COMPOSITION.

FOR A LITTLE GIRL.

A composition good and long
With not a single sentence wrong,
In spite of cloudy morn or night
I must, to please my teacher, write ;
And if I might but choose my plan
And write one such as best I can ;
But size, as well as form, defines
My Master, thus : " At least ten lines."
It is too hard, but here they go—
" Ten lines," and this is all I know !

VISIT OF THE MAGI.

Guided by that mystic star,
  Ne'er by mortals seen before,
Lo ! the Magi from afar
  Come the Saviour to adore !
Lowly bending o'er the spot
  Where the infant Saviour lay,
See them freely pouring out
  Treasures, while they praise and pray :

So, whene'er the Saviour dear,
  Shadowed by that mystic star,
In His precious grace is near,
  Hence to lure thy spirit far,
May you, then, with sweet accord,
  As the Wise-men once before,
Near in spirit to your Lord,
  Lowly bending, Him adore!

LINES ON FAITH.

Faith!—'Tis a precious gift,
  A leading grace I ween—
The SUM of all we hope or seek,
  The SENSE of things not seen!

By IT, the ancient chiefs—
  The faithful and the true,
When wearied by a thousand griefs
  And sorrows ever new—
Each, leaning on this grace,
  A good report obtained!
And, when their life was fled apace,
  O'er death a triumph gained!

Thro' FAITH we understand
  That—Reason O how shamed—
Obedient each to God's command,
  The orbed worlds were framed.
And hence 'tis truly said,
  That objects far and near
Were not as by mechanics made
  Of things which do APPEAR!

By FAITH did Abel bring
A sacrifice APPROVED—
More precious than the gifts of Cain
Who ne'er his Maker loved ;
By which he likewise gained
A witness fair and good,
That HE a righteous man was found,
With God in favor stood !

By FAITH was Enoch spared
The cruel pangs of death
Translated by the God of grace,
Nor yielding up his breath ;
For he—and Oh ! how blest—
Had, ere from earth released,
The cheering witness in his breast,
His Maker that he pleased !

But when, of FAITH devoid,
Proud mortals here below
Approach the God of Holiness,
'Tis all an empty show ;
For God, without THIS grace,
We mortals cannot please,
Since he, who comes to God, must feel
God IS—a God of Peace !

By FAITH did Noah—warned
Of things not seen as yet,
And moved by fear—prepare an ark
And so the danger met ;
By which, the wicked world
Was doomed to endless shame,
And HE an heir of righteousness
By faith in God became !

By FAITH, when he was called,
Did Abraham depart—
And so the voice of God obeyed
The man of pious heart—
Scarce knowing where to go,
Yet ceased not to believe
That HE the bright inheritance
Should afterward receive !

By FAITH sojourning lone,
The country he surveyed—
There dwelt a stranger with his son,
The heir of Promise made ;
For he a city sought
With basis firm and broad,
Whose BUILDER is the Sov'reign Lord,
The ever-living God !

Faith !—'Tis a precious gift,
A leading grace I ween—
The SUM of all we hope or seek
The SENSE of things not seen !

BE CONTENT.

Things are transient here below,
Joys incessant come and go,
Pleasures here are ALL we know,
   Mixed with woe !

Still each season kindly brings
With its bitter, sweetest things,
Many a bird with drooping wings,
   Sweetly sings !

Glad the limpid waters flow
In their channels meek and low,
Nor a plaintive feeling show
                    As they go !

So, too, speak in notes of love
Voices from the field and grove,
And the starry hosts above
                    As they rove !

LINES FOR LIZZIE.

ONE, me-thinks—of tender age,
Glancing o'er this printed page,
Will discern a promise here,
Hasty made and yet sincere,
Now, tho' somewhat after time,
Cleverly discharg'd in rhyme.

And, as I do chiefly write
For this little merry sprite,
She will surely here discern
And a lesson meekly learn—
Learn how freely Jesus loves,
And each humble soul approves !

He, by Angel-bands on high
Praised beyond the vaulted sky,
In Himself supremely bless'd,
And of every joy possessed—
Leaves the shining seats above
And descends on wings of love !

When on earth he lived and moved,
Christ " the little children" loved—

Did the tender lambs embrace
And on them bestow His grace;
Now He pleads for them above,
High in yonder world of love!

Like the Saviour, mild and meek,
Children should His blessing seek,
Love their little playmates dear
And each sinful action fear;
Jesus will their HELPER prove,
Full of mercy—full of love!

Cheerful, loving, brisk and gay,
Children should devoutly pray—
Bend the knee, and lift the eye
Up to Him who rules on high;
Thus in humble faith adore
Christ who loves us evermore!

TO MY WIFE.

Fairest of the fair on earth,
Noble in thy mien and birth,
. Child of deep and tender love,
Partner of the pure above—
In thy meek and placid face,
True affection I can trace—
Of the dear and precious few,
Dearest to my heart are you!

When my soul in sadness wails,
And each fond affection fails;
When the sky looks dark and drear,
And no star doth there appear;

Then I gaze on thee and know
ONE is faithful here below—
Of the dear and precious few,
Dearest to my heart are you!

Joined in bonds of purest love,
By the Lord who reigns above,
We are one in heart and soul,
And submit to His control—
With me thou dost tread the road
Which conducts us up to God—
Of the dear and precious few,
Dearest to my heart are you!

THEY ALL SAY SO!

I saw a little infant blest,
    All innocence and glee,
Reclining on its mother's breast,
    Sit on its mother's knee,
And on that little infant's face
    I read the sentence plain :
The burthen of this mortal life
    Is—sorrow, grief, and pain!

I saw a child of riper years,
    More sportive still than this,
And in its little eyes there beamed
    An over-flowing bliss ;
Yet ever and anon it spake
    In simple, childlike strain :
The burthen of this mortal life
    Is—sorrow, grief and pain!

I saw a youth of finest form,
  With spirits strong and high,
Life seemed to him a pleasant dream,
  A constant flow of joy;
But on his manly brow I traced
  The mark of sin's domain:
The burthen of this mortal life
  Is—sorrow, grief, and pain!

I saw a yet more lovely maid,
  With blushing cheeks and fair,
Her eye was full of tend'rest love,
  Her heart as light as air;
Yet she—the sweet and lovely maid
  Could not the sigh restrain:
The burthen of this mortal life
  Is—sorrow, grief, and pain!

I saw a man of riper age,
  Full thirty years and ten,
Whose visage fair and noble mien
  Gave vigor to my pen;
Yet as I wrote him "happy" down,
  He cried—in sad refrain:
The burthen of this mortal life
  Is—sorrow, grief, and pain!

I saw an aged pilgrim now,
  With silv'ry locks and gray,
And heard him, leaning on his staff,
  With deep emotion say:
" Lo! infancy and childhood fair,
  And youth and age complain:
The burthen of this mortal life
  Is—sorrow, grief, and pain!"

DEDICATION FOR AN ALBUM.

This "Album" is a "garden-plot"—where love
Doth nourish plants descended from above,
Where flow'rets, decked with beauty and with grace,
A genial soil may find—a welcome place ;
Where ev'ry virtue thrives and vice disarms ;
Where sinless love displays its sweetest charms ;
Where innocence and beauty may combine
A fadeless "wreath" for FRIENDSHIP's brow to twine !

Come, Patrons, write upon this snowy sheet,
In verse or prose, some lines with love replete ;
And let this "ALBUM," tho' not wholly "white,"
Betray no hateful tho't in what you write ;
'Tis FRIENDSHIP's Album called, and should be pure
As gold in furnace tried ; nor ever 'lure
The unwary feet and guileless heart of youth
Save to the sparkling fount of love and truth !

WELCOME TO MY REDEEMER.

ADVENT HYMN.

" Welcome, welcome, dear Redeemer,
Welcome to this heart of mine ;"
Be Thou mine and mine forever,
And my soul forever Thine—
Thine, O Saviour,
Thine forever,
Be this ransomed heart of mine !

" Welcome, welcome, dear Redeemer.
Welcome to this heart of mine ;"
Be my life, my light, and glory,
Let Thy light within me shine—
Light of heaven,
Kindly given,
Shine, within my bosom, shine !

" Welcome, welcome, dear Redeemer,
Welcome to this heart of mine ;"
Take, O take me, Lord, forever,
Thine I am and only Thine—
None shall ever,
'Tween us sever,
I am Thine and Thou art mine !

MINISTERS OF CHRIST.

O, for the Heroes, firm and strong,
To preach God's word, divinely called,
Endued with power to dare the wrong,
Nor by men's blust'ring threats appalled ;
With tongues of fire and hearts of love,
May they proclaim Thy saving Word,
And, kindly aided from above,
May sinners bow before Thee, Lord !

THE ANGEL-GREETING.

The sky was bathed in lovliest hues,
And moon and stars were sweetly mute,
And whisp'rings, soft as sounds of lute,
Came, mingling with the falling dews—

An Angel, from that brilliant zone,
    Iu glory swept athwart the plain ;
And radiant hosts their Chief did own,
    Aud, rapt, broke forth in sweetest strain,
Exultant shouting—as they sang—
    " To God Most High be glory given"—
" And peace on earth, good-will to men,"
Responsive, still the chorus rang !

NEW-YEAR'S ADDRESS.

I come, your faithful Carrier-boy, once more,
    My Patrons. on this New-year's morn, to greet ;
I wish you, now, as I have done before,
    Much joy—a long, long life with bliss replete ;
I wish you health, and pious friends and kind,
    Whate'er of good, or Time or Earth can give—
I wish you peace with God—a Saviour's mind,
    And with Him, in His peerless joy, to live !

The Law of Carrier-boys—'tis said by men—
Compels them, once a year, to use their pen ;
The Rule is wise, and serves a purpose high,
It gives a chance their growing strength to try.
'Tis true, great dangers also meet the young,
And pit-falls lie the shining path along—
The MEEK, the rose-bud opens to adorn,
But warns th' aspiring, to beware the thorn !

I know it—'Tis ambition's pow'r that sways
The fickle world with all its foolish ways ;
Each in his turn doth painted honors seek,
Th' aspiring proud, and e'en the seeming meek ;

The humblest often craves a wreath of fame,
And on the solid rock inscribes his name;
Each recent fashion, style, or mode of life,
All are but forms with rank ambition rife!

Such is the world—Its virtues idle seem,
And all its boasted works are but a dream.
The deeds of men, thus, wear a double face,
In form attractive, but in essence base;
But o'er this vain and fleeting world there is,
What shall we say? a scene of perfect bliss;
And all my weekly rounds, and anxious care,
But for this highest good—incite—prepare!

What have I brought you in each weekly call?
What messages alike for each—for all?—
Was not the burden of my song, each week,
Repent of sin—your loving Saviour seek?
Did not each sheet, I carried to your door,
Contain some comfort for the humble poor?
And was not, also, for the HAUGHTY there
A word of warning to arouse his fear?

I know full well, my efforts are but weak,
And imperfection, in each line, bespeak;
I fear not to confess this common shame,
Or ask forgiveness in a Saviour's name;
'Tis better far to learn our follies here,
And o'er them shed the penitential tear,
Than HIDE our sin, and in our blindness boast,
Till, in the final wreck, our souls be lost!

With thoughts like these impressed, I came
A " Messenger" of peace; and, in God's name,
Did warn the wicked of his ways perverse,
And, in his ears, the coming doom rehearse;

The HUMBLE I did cheer; and, when afraid,
A soothing balm upon his heart I laid ;
Pointed poor sinners to the " Lamb of God,"
With hopes of pardon in atoning blood !

Still more—I led the blind in Virtue's way,
And gave directions how to praise and pray ;
To read God's holy Word with profit—how
The soul must to its precepts humbly bow ;
I warned, against delusions, young and old,
And how these nets to shun I often told ;
No single law or precept, that I knew,
For want of forethought left I out of view !

How often, on some wintry eve, I've taught
Sweet truth, by parents and by children sought !
The blithesome group around the table sat,
And read—the one loved this, the other that.
For each one, thus, a little crumb I brought,
And each his own by far the sweetest thought ;
Then, at the close, they read the sacred Word,
Around the Altar knelt, and blessed the Lord !

" Amen"—so each one, with the father, said,
And then arose, and hastened off to bed ;
The night gave rest—'twas not too short nor long,
The weary limbs relaxed, and then grew strong ;
The spirit—calm, confiding in its God—
Beneath His shadow found a safe abode ;
And o'er the bed, and 'round it angels stood,
From ill defending, and bestowing good !

When, by and by, the morn began to dawn,
Ere Sol's bright rays had kissed the dewy lawn,
Refreshed and quickened by their sweet repose,
They all, from oldest down to youngest, 'rose ;

And, trained most fitly by parental care,
Each offered up its simple morning pray'r;
Then, cheerful, each unto his labor sped,
And ceaseless wrought until the day was fled!

I may not claim, as many seem to claim,
Some special praise, or honors to my name;
Yet, as a " Messenger" from God, I brought
A pious mind, and so these wonders wrought :
For, love to God, and love to man, I ween,
As factors, in each pious work, are seen ;
And "godliness" secures, as taught by some,
The present life, and THAT which is to come!

Of praise so far as this is due to men—
I claim, and justly claim a portion then.
My weekly calls, I made from door to door,
The rich I pleased—I cheered the humble poor,
And all my labors, done in purest love,
Sought, first of all, to fix the heart above;
And, now, with each one's highest good in view,
I bid you, patrons, ALL a kind ADIEU!

LOVE AND HATE.

Two sprightly lasses, young and gay,
Met oftentimes to frisk and play,
And just as often as they met,
The one of them got in a pet—
Sweet Amie always kept so cool,
That Spitie called her ape and fool |

She bore the insult, meek and kind,
And quarrels Spitie could not find ;

One day sweet Amie said of Love
That it descended from above,
And Spitie said : my Hate, I know,
Hails from the regions dark below.

At this confession Amie smiled,
But Spitie saw her and reviled !
The little creature, meek and mild,
Said, kindly chiding, "hush my child."
The visage grim of Spitie grew
Pale, at this word, and red and blue.

Poor Amie feared or fist or palm,
Yet, conscious of her right, was calm ;
And Spitie, seeing Love so strong,
Confessed to Amie all her wrong ;
Their hearts—cemented into one—
Bore witness of this wonder done !

Now oft the lasses, young and gay,
Meet LOVINGLY to frisk and play.
And so the story—they relate—
Shows Love superior far to Hate ;
The peerless virtue from above,
Triumphant over Hate, is—LOVE !

SOMETHING FOR CHILDREN.

The little folks, so bright and gay,
Who read the "HELPER," sing, and pray,
   Are children truly wise ;
If, as they read, and sing, and pray,
They also walk in Wisdom's way,
   Conducting to the skies !

The " HELPER" gently moves the heart,
From sin, and death, and hell to part,
  And seek its home above ;
It drives away the shades of night,
And kindles there a sacred light—
  The light of life and love!

And little folks, so richly blest,
With means of sacred joy and rest,
  Are children blest indeed ;
They live a life of peace below,
Nor bitter tears above shall know,
  Nor any painful need !

Then, children, come—all bright and gay,
Come read the " HELPER," sing, and pray,
  Be children truly wise ;
And, as you read, and sing, and pray,
Walk briskly on in Wisdom's way,
  Still upward to the skies !

OUR SAINTED LOVED ONES.

FOR MR. AND MRS. W. B. B.

'Twas quiet on that eve of fate,
When, thoughtful, sat we, and sedate ;
And, then, a tap—strong tapping at the door,
That knock, we tho't, tho' strange, was heard before,
But LOUDER, now, it seemed, and cruel more ;
  And each one felt a painful thrill
  Yet, stricken, we were still—were still !

Time passed, and cheeks, once rosy-bright,
Were strangely dimpled now with white ;
But, then, in sweet and tender notes we heard
That strangely soothing, soft, and magic word,
The blessed, soothing word of Christ—the Lord ;
    And, then, we bowed, in silence bowed,
    And to our Lord submission vowed !

Again we heard a whisp'ring sweet,
For angel tongues and voices meet ;
And far away, in that bright spirit-land,
There, happy, stood the twain with angel-band ;
And, then, in triumph each one waved the hand ;
    And, thus, we knew—knew what it meant,
    Removed were they whom God had lent !

And often, now, as vent'rous fancy paints
The joys supreme of rescued saints,
We seem, in rapt'rous notes again to hear
Sweet voices, gently, softly, strike the ear ;
And so the charming song continues near,
    Still floating—quiv'ring on the air,
    In measured accents, sweet and fair !

And, O, how soon that call shall come,
Which welcomes all to yon sweet home !
When, joyous, we, with all the sainted dead,
Shall, rescued, stand before the bar so dread,
And, clothed in Christ, the Church's living Head,
    Be joined with saints of fair renown,
    And, with them, wear th' immortal crown !

What glorious prospects, fair and bright,
Await us in that world of light !
The blessed saints, from all their failings free,
Shall there, enrapt, the King of glory see ;

And, then, in Him exulting, bend the knee,
And, so, with hosts of angels bright,
Shall bask in seas of living light!

THE GOOD MAN'S LIFE.

The good man dies, indeed, but leaves behind
    The strong, sweet savor of a holy life ;
His earnest faith, and love, and labors find
    A mellow soil with vital forces rife ;
Where ownward, even to the latest hour,
They live to work in secret, silent, power!

THE SERVANTS OF CHRIST.

And who are they that claim to be
    Commissioned from above,
To preach alike to bond and free
    God's sweet and boundless love ?

Heralds of Christ, in mercy sent
    Glad tidings to proclaim—
Th' unrighteous urging to repent
    And trust in Jesus' name ;
While, to the penitent, they speak
    Sweet words of pardon—peace ;
And kindly urge them all to seek
    From sin a full release !

O, what a wondrous work is theirs,
    Their calling—O how high !
Of life, in Christ, to make men heirs,
    Proclaim salvation nigh ;

The words of peace to mourners speak,
    To comfort the distrest—
To proffer healing to the sick,
    And to the weary—rest!

Then, when their kindly work is done,
    They lay their armor down,
And, mounting to the exalted throne,
    Receive th' immortal crown!

LINES ON THE FABLE OF THE RAIN DROPS.

FIRST VERSION.

Just as the little rain-drops
    Came patt'ring on the ground,
To cheer the saddened farmer,
    Whom in the field they found;
Uniting all their forces,
    And hast'ning down below,
The arid soil was moistened,
    The corn was made to grow.

So, too, should little children,
    In pity and in love—
Like gentle rain distilling
    Rich blessings from above—
Unite their kindly off'rings,
    Their efforts evermore,
And shower daily blessings
    Upon the humble poor.

SECOND VERSION.

Just as the rain-drops and the dew
    Rejoiced the farmer—cheered his soil;

So should the little children, too,
Make glad the poor—relieve their toil!

Each one alone not much can give,
But, if ONE gives, then others will;
And so they can the poor relieve,
As many waters turn the mill!

Each little gift—a dime, a cent,
Will of the treasure make a part;
And trifles, thus, in mercy lent,
Will greatly bless and cheer the heart!

"THY WILL BE DONE."

When stern affliction's hand is laid
Upon this frame of mine,
And woes, in deepest gloom arrayed,
Against me thus combine—
Then, Father, to Thy throne on high
In faith I lift my tearful eye,
And say: Thy will be done!

When o'er me comes disaster bleak,
And riches take them wings—
Fly swift away as lightning streak,
And grief each moment brings—
Then, O' my God, to Thee I look,
Thus bravely each misfortune brook,
And say: Thy will be done!

When foes in mighty mass combine,
And friends grow faint and few—
When every tort'ring pain is mine,
And tears mine eyes bedew—

Then, Father, to Thy hand benign.
Composed, do I myself resign,
    And say : Thy will be done !

When silent grief my bosom heaves,
    My heart with anguish wrung—
When sorrow not a moment leaves
    The trembling nerves unstrung—
Then, O my God, still fost'ring me,
I lift my burthened soul to Thee,
    And say : Thy will be done !

When weary with the cares of life,
    By constant woe pressed down—
When each blest day, with sorrow rife.
    Brings me a thorny crown—
Then, Father, in Thy wise decree
Assured, I lift my soul to Thee,
    And say : Thy will he done !

When prostrate on my couch I lie,
    And hope my breast forsakes—
When languid grows my fixed eye,
    And life of gloom partakes—
Then, Saviour, in Thy purple tide
Still calmly shall my soul confide,
    And say : Thy will be done !

When death, at length, with sable wing
    Spreads darkness o'er my soul—
When love nor friendship aid can bring,
    Nor skill the tide control—
Then, Father, by the Spirit's breath,
Sustained, I triumph e'en in death,
    And say : Thy will be done !

ALLES IST EITEL—EIN TRAUM.

In einer Nacht, gar heiss und schwuel,
  Lag ich auf meinem Bette,
Mein Herz war voll von Schwergefuehl,
  Mein Geist in einer Kette,
Da traeumte mir, ich reiste hin
  Wo frueher ich mal wohnte.
Besuchte meiner Freunde viel,
  Und treu' mit treu' belohnte.

Da schien's als ob sie gaeben mir
  Sehr herrliche Geschenke;
Der eine bringt Goldmuenzen viel
  Und legt sie mir in Haende;
Der and're bringt mir Kleidstueck' dar
  Mit grosser Mueh' bereitet;
Eiu dritter macht den Weg mir klar,
  Mich hie und da begleitet.

So ging's—ich fuehlte mich beglueckt,
  Weil Freunde viel mir dienten;
Doch, ach!—ich wurde fast verrueckt,
  Der Stolz blieb nicht dahinten;
Mein Herr, der alles sieht und weiss,
  Sah meine schlimme Lage;
Und hoerte nun, zwar sanft und leis,
  Auch meine bitt're Klage.

Da lies Er, auf dem schoenen Weg,
  Mich viele Leut' begleiten,
Und, so, durch einen, im Gespraech,
  Mir Licht und Heil bereiten:
Der sprach, als ich ihm nahe war,
  Zu einem auf der Strasse;
"Wir brachten ihm sehr vieles dar,
  Hat Schuld in gleichem Masse."

"So"—dachte ich in meinem Traum,
  "So geht's bei solchen Leuten;
Sie geben zwar, doch geben kaum,
  So sucht man schon die beuten."
Nun sah ich um—erbluockte da
  Ein Wunder-strom entquellen,
Und, in demselben, grosse Schaar
  Der Fische schoen—Forellen!

"Nun fang ich die," so dachte ich,
  "Und habe Freud die Fuelle;"
Dann, eilends Wuermer suchte ich
  Am Strom in aller stille;
Und als ich war voll Koth and dreck,
  Wie man die Fischer findet,
So geht mir auch mein Schlaf hinweg,
  Mein schoener Traum verschwindet!

Nun sah ich in dem Traum ein Bild
  Der Menschen Gunst und Liebe;
Die Leute geben frei und mild
  Aus scheinbar reinem Triebe;
Doch ist's, wenn man dahinter koemmt,
  Nur Tand und eitle Sache,
Die sprache, die vom Munde stroemt,
  Its voll von Trug und Rache!

Und sucht man, wie im schoenen Strom,
Die Freude in der Stille,
Und denkt, da gibt es doch gewiss
Ein Glueck nach Wunsch und Wille,
So findet man das Fluesse schoen
Das Glueck zwar in uns wecken,
Doch, eh' wir es errungen seh'n,
Bleibt man im Kothe stecken!

O, gluecklich sind—die nur allein
Auf Gott, nicht Menschen, trauen,
Die, in des Lebens Freud und Pein,
Auf Gottes Grade bauen—
Hier findet keine Taeuschung statt,
Bewaehrt ist Glueck und Wonne,
Hier bleibt was man gehoffet hat,
Gott selbst ist "Schild und Sonne."

THE HOME ABOVE.

There is for weary souls a Home,
A rest from all their toils and cares ;
A House whence saints no more shall roam,
A place wherein each pilgrim shares ;
To this dear "home"—this rest above—
Are gathered all the sons of love!

INSCRIPTION.

FIRST FORM.

Little Pilgrim, thou art sleeping
Softly sleeping in the ground ;
Angels o'er thee vigils keeping,
Vigils keeping all around—

Gently, sweetly, thus reposing,
    All thy weary wand'rings o'er,
Hail we thee—" Asleep iu Jesus"—
    Happy, happy—evermore !

SECOND FORM.

Little Pilgrim, thou art sleeping,
    Softly sleeping 'neath the sod ;
Angels o'er thee vigils keeping,
    Vigils keeping near thy God—
Safely, sweetly now reposing,
    All thy weary wand'rings o'er,
Hail we thee—" Asleep in Jesus"—
    Hail thee happy evermore !

ON LOSING A CHECK SENT BY MAIL.

TO REV. M. A. S.

Dear Sir—I share your present grief,
And fain would send you kind relief,
With many a heart-felt wish, that you
May, undisturbed, your course pursue.

Enclosed, please find another " scrip,'
May IT not, likewise, give the slip ;
But serve to pay the honest " tax,"
Et tibi, nunc, sit magna pax !

Ich schreib in Englisch und Latein,
Deweil du bist ein " scholar" fein,
Und kannst gewiss auch schaetzen das
Was ich dir schreib in lauter Spass.

Here goes my letter with its scrip,
For which I crave a pleasant trip ;

Do thou, Dear Sir, the message hail,
And pay the "custom" without fail !

LINES FOR AN AUTOGRAPH ALBUM.

These " Autographs" be pure and bright,
And free from what is low and vile ;
Be sure that what you here do write
May not the spotless page defile !

Here Friends should gather flow'rets sweet,
To shed their fragrance o'er the page,
And each contribute, what is meet,
To foster love from age to age !

Then write with prudence and with taste,
Lest Virtue weep and Scorners laugh ;
May, always, what is pure and chaste
Distinctly mark each Autograph !

ALIENATION OF MY SIGNATURE.

Do, Sir, Editor, please take note,
That one, from baseness tho' remote,
Employs of late a subscript name
Which I by right of usage claim.
The guardian of my rights are YOU,
Then to your TRUST be firm and true ;
Rebuke the act, in language strong,
And save me, thus, from further wrong.
The guilty one, please, gently tap,
Or sternly o'er the knuckles rap ;

Thus may you what is past amend,
And to my FAITH yourself commend.
The subject, now, I leave with you,
Assured you will be firm and true,
And do me justice in the case,
Despite the noble or the base!

TO THE OFFENDER.

And, now, I turn to you,
   Sir master of the quill;
I claim my honest due,
   Respect my wish and will.
There's sure no LETTER dearth,
   In choice you've ample room ;
Why then, in name of earth,
   Purloin my " Nom de Plume."
Of twenty points and six
   Select your needed three,
But leave ME still affix
   My own dear " X—Y—Z."

THE KATYDID.

'Tis often harder than you think
To locate Nature's ev'ry link—
E'en this wee thing of rustic suit
Has gendered many a fierce dispute ;
For, while some few, self-rated high,
Repute the insect flat as pie,
Some others, with far keener wit,
" Concavum" call my—Katydid!

This settled, we may now unite
To magnify this little sprite,   -
It seldom sings in June or May,
And night prefers to sunny day ;

The male alone in song excells,
Nor he nor she the reason tells,
And ask you, who the secret hid,
Sweet Echo answers—Katydid !

Thus things are oft eccentric found,
And Nature's law is shifted round,
For, here, unlike in grades above,
The Beau sings to his Lady-love ;
And tho' he sings this plaintive air
"Who loved me ?' to his maiden fair,
She—roguishly in ambush hid—
Respondeth not Miss—Katydid !

Ye little creatures serve to show
The habits current here below,
And foibles, even, strange and new,
In higher natures brought to view ;
So—of mankind the coy and fair
With this sly imp may we compare ;
For, oft some blushing MAID hath hid,
This likewise did, my—Katydid !

When Summer, with its swelt'ring heat,
Gives way to Autumn, sober, sweet,
And days grow short, and ev'nings long,
Then hear we oft their plaintive song,
As sings the disappointed maid
When by her faithless beau betrayed ;
But what the maids in beaus have chid,
That same did she, my—Katydid !

And, now, what tribute shall we bring,
To this dear, pretty, little thing ?
So quaint and odd in every way,
It sings at night, and rests by day ;

So modest, in its suit of green,
Thro' all the week the thing is seen ;
'Twere well if ALL of pride were rid,
And dressed and lived as—Katydid !

"PEARL OF THE PARK."

There is a Place, enshrined in living green,
And fairer aught the eye hath seldom seen,
A charming spot—it matters not just where
The fairy scene is found ; but, surely there
The heart, elate, with forms of beauty charmed,
In pleasures rev'ling, yet is left unharmed.
The stately pine, in fadeless verdure drest,
Uplifting, waves aloft its beauteous crest ;
Beneath its spreading limbs and cooling shade
The laurel thrives, in emerald suit arrayed,
With blooming chaplet crowned of richest hue,
And fraught with pleasures rare for me and you.
'Mid tangled vines, and creepers wild and bare,
Luxuriant, green, and decked with flow'rets fair,
The fragrant spice-wood grows, of eld renowned,
In regal style with scarlet berries crowned ;
And 'neath the whole, and 'mid the mantling green,
The laughing brooks and sparkling rills are seen ;
And, nimbly dancing thro' the wilds profound,
Display their sweetest charms—shed music round.
Low, on the humid earth a humbler train
Of gorgeous mosses and of lichens plain ;
The sweet arbutus, trailing on the ground,
And winter-green, so fragrant, there are found ;
In thickets dank, the curious eye discerns
A train of modest, yet majestic ferns.
And there in festoons swung on tow'ring trees,

The grape vines, clust'ring round, one often sees ;
There, too, the hazel, with its tasseled host,
Grows lank and tall, the marsh's pride and boast ;
The fragrant birch, its bark with sweetness rife,
Oft tempts a peeling from the youngster's knife,
Who, whittling, doth God's fairest works deface,
And, thus, in shame involves our boasting race !
Amid the dazzling scenes of trees and vines,
An emerald hedge a fountain pure enshrines ;
The grateful shade, within that cool retreat,
The trav'ler tempts to rest his weary feet ;
And, gazing on the limpid streamlets there,
With eyes still doting on each scene so fair,
Athirst, well-pleased he dips the waters up,
And to his lips conveys the sparkling cup.
All o'er the woods, and in the forest round,
The wild birds sing, and noblest game is found.
On loftiest pines the wary gobbler sleeps,
Or, waking, o'er his charge strict vigil keeps ;
The timid partridge, erstwhile pheasant named,
Flies whirring past, and foils the gunner famed :
The speckled trout—so exquisitely fair—
Sports in the purling brook, with antics rare,
Or, in some sheltered nook, doth coyly lie   .
Th' unwary bug to snatch, or moth, or fly ;
Rare birds—of plumage fair. and golden wing,
Their sweet and charming songs incessant sing.
'Tis, there, unharmed in that sequestered spot,
That weeping ones have oft their woes forgot ;
'Tis, there, remote from earth's incessant toil,
The wounded spirit finds a soothing oil—
'Mid scenes so fair, they roam serene and calm,
And find in Nature's stores the healing balm !
How often, too, have I strayed, musing, there,
And solace found when vexed with tort'ring care.

Sweet, sacred spot, entranced I think of thee,
And, ruminant in thought, thy beauties see !
There, too, the young, with spirits light and gay,
In pleasant converse oft have spent the day ;
Around the trees, and 'neath their foliage green,
In playful groups arranged, they oft are seen ;
And motly crowds, from scattered hamlets round,
In rural sports engaged—are likewise found.
Both old and young in friendly concourse met,
Are happier made, and all their cares forget !
But, chiefly, gathered round the crystal spring,
In cheerful mood, they frisk, and play, and sing ;
Their clarion voices ring the trees among,
And rocks and hills reverberate the song.
Then, weary and athirst, they haste to greet
The sparkling fount, and quaff its waters sweet;
The cooling draft revives their spirits faint,
Imparts new life, and hinders all complaint.
Sweet sparkling fount ! how rich thy dolings are,
Of sylvan gifts the best—the richest far !
For ALL things, that, while wand'ring here below,
Men, in their wildest dreams, or think or know,
Are little prized, and of but small account,
When, thirsty, they espy the sparkling fount ;
The echoing woods with shouts of triumph ring,
And, hast'ning, each one greets the crystal spring !
What pleasant things are said of thee, sweet spot,
May, in the world's confusion, be forgot,
But mem'ry still the impress deep enshrines,
And, as its rarest treasure, there confines.
What generous heart can e'er forget the spell
That binds the spirit to that forest dell ?
The purling brooks and "thousand" springlets clear,
And shaded groves and lone retreats, so dear—
The floral wreaths and crowns of living green,

And nameless beauties, all, which there are seen ;
These ALL, and each in its peculiar sphere,
Entrance the soul, and make the spot more dear ;
And, so, these charming sights and beauties rare,
In brilliant plots arranged, all bright and fair,
Invest the place with special sense, I ween,
And fix in changeless souls this forest scene !

THE WHIP-POOR-WILL.

Sweet bird of Song, or scold, or both,
Which to decide I'm somewhat loath ;
For, tho' thy presence welcome be,
And thy sweet song is full of glee,
Yet, something in that song, my lord,
Doth not with mercy well accord ;
For, sing you on the plain or hill,
You cease not calling—"Whip-poor-will."

Sweet bird of Song ! In early Spring,
We hear thy voice around us ring,
And here and there on stump or stone,
Thou sweetly singest all alone ;
And, hence, thy song I much admire,
So full of vim—so full of fire ;
To one thing though object I will,
Thy loveless shouting—"Whip-poor-will."

Sweet bird of Song ! Not sweet alone,
But useful thee we, likewise, own,
On insect hosts, all sleek and fine,
Dost thou at night both sup and dine ;
For all, who know thee, well do ken,
That, in despite of beasts or men,
Thou dost by night secure thy fill,
While sweetly singing—"Whip-poor-will."

Sweet bird of Song! I hear them ring—
Thy sweet and mellow notes of spring,
And who that kens thy sylvan muse,
Would thee a tribute glad refuse ;
For what could fill our hearts with cheer,
If 'twere not for thy voice so clear?
Thy song—despite the painful thrill,
Is sweet, tho' saying—"Whip-poor-will."

Sweet bird of Song! In fall or spring,
I love to hear thee near me sing,
Nor can I e'er forget thy strain,
Loud-echoing, still, o'er hill and plain ;
Hence, glad, will I my tribute pay
To him that sleeps the live long day,
And sings at night, so calm and still,
His own clear-ringing—"Whip-poor-will."

Sweet bird of Song! I'm much in doubt,
And greatly wish you'd help me out—
I've called thee "lord," but am afraid
You are some disappointed maid ;
Else, why alone poor "Will," thus, hate ?
Nor Sue, nor Mag, nor Lib, nor Kate ?
Nor thine invectives e'er abate ?
For sing you, bird, on plain or hill,
'Tis still, and only—"Whip-poor-will."

Sweet bird of Song! who art thou, then,
That we thy story well may ken !
For not a "lord," but maiden fair
May sing this song of deep despair ;
Me pardon, for I much suspect
'Tis vengeance for some sore neglect ;
For sing you, bird, or loud or still,
'Tis thus, and ALWAYS—"Whip-poor-will,"

TO MY NIECE.

I've read the Letter which you sent
To L. R. H. 'Twas to me lent ;
Quite glad was I to hear of you,
Of all you did, or MEANT to do ;
'Tis pleasant, thus, to read one's mind,
And learn if she be cross or kind ;
For, secrets got with little cost,
Are longest kept, and rarely lost !
I cannot tell you ALL I've read,
Too many things distract my head ;
But one thing I will here repeat,
Which was to me a pleasant treat.
A flatt'ring word of praise, I ween,
In your Epistle I have seen—
Your ref'rence to my rhyming art
Responsive touched my mind and heart ;
And, then, the wish that I might woo
The Maid poetic, pleased me too ;
For, wooing, as you well do know,
Is current with the high and low ;
And well becomes the good and true,
If they but nobler ends pursue.
Now, viewing things in such a light,
With matters all so fair and bright,
I cannot well your wish refuse,
To court, at times, the Sacred Muse ;
The end proposed is lofty, sure,
And, deeming it both good and pure,

I'll visit oft her charming fane,
To please my Niece—Miss Mary Jane!

THE GOLDEN WEDDING.

FEB. 10, 1879.

Our Hearts conjoined—together grown,
As sketched, and by this emblem* shown,
Glad, sing we still Life's path along,
In sweet content our pilgrim song!

We bless Thee, Lord, for life and health,
We bless Thee for our friends and wealth,
We bless Thee for each gift of Thine,
We bless Thee for Thy grace divine!

With wondrous love, and matchless skill,
Thou dost Thy gracious word fulfill;
From day to day—from year to year,
Thou dost our drooping spirits cheer!

Through dangers oft our journey lay,
Thro' these Thy hand hath led the way;
Thro' shifting scenes of storm and calm,
Thro' sweetly scented groves of balm!

O wondrous grace! O bliss divine!
To know that all our cares are Thine;
Thy light, at midnight, gleams on high,
In gloomiest days, Thy help is nigh!

THE FESTIVE ODE.

Sweet songs of joy, sweet songs of praise,
With cheerful heart and voice we'll raise
To Him—the High, the Pure, the Good,
Who giveth life, and health, and food!

*Two hearts in one.

To Thee, the blessed God, we bring
Our grateful off'rings while we sing,
Our hearts attuned to scenes above,
Our tongues intoning notes of love!

With firmness, Lord, our souls inspire,
And touch our lips with sacred fire;
Our sweetest notes to Thee we'll raise,
To Thee intone our loftiest praise!

Our pilgrimage, so bright and fair,
Doth witness to Thy mercy bear;
And, when distressed with doubt and fear,
Thy hand removes the falling tear!

We bless, O Lord, Thy hand benign,
And to Thy grace ourselves resign;
What suited off'ring shall we bring?
What worthy Anthem shall we sing?

We'll praise Thee, Lord, in grateful song,
We'll praise Thee, Lord, with heart and tongue;
We'll praise Thee for each favor showed,
We'll praise Thee for each gift bestowed!

Sweet anthems, then, sweet songs of praise,
With cheerful voices, we will raise
To Thee, the weary pilgrims stay,
ON THIS OUR GOLDEN-WEDDING DAY!

THE OLIVE TREE.

Sweet Olive tree—of stature small,
    With knarled trunk and modest mien,
And, yet, so rich in gifts for all—
    The pride and boast of Palestine.

On ev'ry hill and mountain side
    The precious trees in mass are found,
And, there, in freshness they abide
    While seasons, each, come circling round.

Sweet evergreen, of changeless leaf,
    Of verdure fresh thro' all the year,
The emblem of that glorious Chief,
    The Lord of life, to mortals dear.
How blithely to my heart and mind
    It speaks of Him who came to save,
The Lord and Head of human-kind,
    Who wreathed the cross—illumed the grave!

Far in the dim and hoary past,
    When o'er the angry waters rode
The Ark all safe—tho' rough and fast,
    Till on the mountain it abode.;
The Dove sent o'er the wat'ry waste,
    A verdant branch of olive found,
And winging back in eager haste,
    She brought the news of rising ground!

What beauty in that picture glows
    Which Judah's bard in fancy drew,
When round the board, in festive rows,
    "Like olive plants," sweet children grew;
When pure content was smiling seen,
    The image of a favored home,
And he himself, all fresh and green,
    Dwelled, grateful, 'neath the sacred dome!

So—in the Prophet's vision bright,
    How grandly stand the Olives "two,"
And, still, to feed the sacred light,
    Flows golden oil the branches thro';

The sacred flame is kept aglow
By reason of the trees so nigh,
For rich supplies do ceaseless flow
From golden vases fixed on high !

Sweet trees of yore, still growing sound
Near Salem's walls of ancient fame !
'Tis there, that, bathed in blood, was found
My Saviour of the mystic name ;
" Anointed"—whence all efforts made
Have failed my Olive to destroy !
Blest Tree of Life !—still rich in shade,
In fruit and oil—the source of joy !

For all the good that trees impart,
For all the evils they prevent,
Thou, most, dost merit my poor heart,
Great Olive mine, in mercy sent ;
In field, and dome, and temple grand,
Thy golden oil doth light afford,
And rich and poor thro' all the land,
For Thy kind dolings bless Thee, Lord !

THE CHRISTIAN HOME.

The purest joy that earth can give,
Is found in kindly deeds of love,
'Tis, thus, the blessed Angels live,
And Saints in radiant spheres above ;
But, why, should not the Sons of Earth,
Still struggling in their course below,
Ennobled by their heavenly birth,
In rapture this sweet pleasure know ?

How fair and charming is the sight
 Of children round the social hearth,
Each serving each with sweet delight,
 In token of their common birth ;
Their hearts are to each oth'er true,
 And constant in their flow of peace,
Their joys come with the early dew,
 Nor with the ev'ning twilight cease !

O, blessed scene of Christian love,
 Exempt from anger, hate, and strife,
A scene like those in worlds above,
 Where, freely, reigns immortal life ;
There clouds ne'er sweep athwart the sky,
 Nor storms disturb the sweet repose,
There ev'ry wished-for good is nigh,
 There springs of bounty ne'er do close !

Sweet, sacred spot ! Pure, blessed scene !
 For thee my heart doth greatly long ;
'Tis highest heav'n to me, I ween,
 A balm for every tort'ring wrong ;
Sweet, sacred spot ! I, longing, pant
 In thy blest scenes to share a part ;
To me, dear Lord, this blessing grant,
 And I, to Thee, will yield my heart !

When, thus, our time on earth is spent
 In blissful concord with our friends ;
When life, passed thro' in sweet content,
 At length in radiant glory ends ;
How blest the thought, that then we may
 In peace depart this life of care,
And find a mansion far away—
 A home divinely bright and fair !

OUR LITTLE WINGED PETS.

Little birds, so blithe and gay,
Cheerily ye frisk and play—
Round the cage so nimbly hop,
From the bottom up to top ;
Then adown, again, to feed,
Cutely hulling all the seed ;
'Cross the cage ye fly or skip,
Then the sparkling water sip ;
Thus it fareth all the day—
Eat and drink, and skip and play !
Little beauties, bright are ye,
Full of fun and full of glee,
Spreading, now, the tiny wing,
Then a song of love you sing,
And, while singing, seem to say
Ain't we pretty, blithe, and gay ?
With your modest yellow suit,
With your little eyes so cute,
With your slender legs and feet,
With your voices soft and sweet,
Who doth not your suit admire,
Who doth of your warblings tire ?
Oft, when musing, I surmise
Reason sparkling in your eyes,
Gifted, thus, conclude I hence,
With a higher grade of sense.

In your ev'ry turn, I ween,
Wisdom is in action seen;
In your pranks and ready wits,
Equal quite to Signor Blitz !

Little warblers, lively, gay,
Ye are happy all the day;
Might we but this lesson learn,
Wisdom in your life discern !
Strangely slow to comprehend,
Miss we, thus, th' exalted end ;
Why should ye of golden wing,
Skip and play, and cheerful sing,
Whereas WE of nobler mould,
Often fret, or pout, or scold ?
'Tis a poor, unhappy choice,
That, with far superior voice,
WE do not as cheerful sing,
As ye birds of golden wing !

Gentle songsters, well-inclined,
To your wiry cage confined !
Yielding, thus, to cruel fate,
Stinted in your small estate ;
Oft I sit, and, musing, think
Ye, too, form a needful link
In that chain of being high,
Reaching upward to the sky ;
And, who knows, what honors more
May for you be kept in store !
In the future there doth lie
Many an unsolved mystery ;
We but see the outward ring—
Pierce not to the secret spring ;
Source of action, this, I ween,
Yet by mortals never seen !

Sing, then, little warblers, sing,
Let your voices sweetly ring,
He, who gave you being, will
All His counsel yet fulfill;
By succession, not in grade,
Ye may be immortal made!
Sing ye here so sweetly, grand,
WE sing in that better land;
Thus, our work doth well accord,
High exalting Christ—the Lord;
And each note, from lip or bill,
Sounding through the ages still,
There, accordant, shall combine
In a song of praise divine!

"MOTHER, HOME, AND HEAVEN."

There's magic in that name, so sweet,
  By children used with sacred awe;
The charming sound our lips repeat
  By virtue of an innate law;
With hearts aglow, and tender love,
  We cherish, here, a Mother's name;
And, yonder, in that world above,
  Still hope we to revere the same!

And that dear spot, where she abides,
  We dignify with name of Home,
And deem no other place besides,
  So dear to pilgrims doomed to roam;
For, there, the weary heart reclines
  On her warm bosom filled with love,
And softly, there, in beauty shines
  The light of brighter worlds above!

That mellowed light, that tints the sky,
　　Betokens still auother Home,
Which gently lures the soul on high,
　　And bids the pilgrim cease to roam ;
For, there, our final rest is found,
　　And weary saints sit calmly down ;
While, sharing in the glory round,
　　Each one receives a fadeless crown .

DEDICATION FOR AN AUTOGRAPH ALBUM.

This Album is a garden, bright and fair,
　　Where beauties of the mind and heart may grow ;
A cabinet of treasures—rich and rare—
　　Mementoes, fragrant, and with life aglow.
As blithely from the smooth and placid lake,
　　The radiant sky and clouds are mirrored back
With lineameuts, exact in form and make,
　　Nor e'en the softest tints and features lack ;
So let your sentiments be chaste and pure,
　　Like sparkling gems, and native gold refined,
Nor in this Album write save thoughts mature,
　　Sweet echoes of a chastened heart and mind !

THE REAPERS.

Behold, the Farmer's fair domain,
　　Out-stretching to the distant hills,
Where he, for pleasure, greed, or gain,
　　With care the soil productive tills.

The seed corns, with a gen'rous hand,
　　Now scattered o'er the mellowed soil,

With verdure clothe the favored land,
Responsive to the farmer's toil.

And, stretching o'er the cultured fields,
Now gently waves the golden grain ;
And, rip'ning, it profusely yields,
Prospective, rich returns of gain !

The em'rald acres, changed to gold,
Invite the reapers to their task,
And they, responding, fresh and bold,
Their garments doff—nor question ask.

Then, hast'ning to the golden fields,
With sickle, scythe, and firm resolve,
The tott'ring grain, responsive, yields
As, now, the serrate wheels revolve !

And, gath'ring up the prostrate grain,
Their lab'ring teams, o'er-laden, quake,
While gleaners, in a num'rous train,
With dear esteem the leavings take !

Away they store these gifts in haste,
The gen'rous dole the garner fills ;
Elate, the gifts of God they taste,
And joy the heaving bosom thrills !

Thus, in the heav'nly kingdom, too,
The seeds of truth are broad-cast sown ;
And, fiilled with virtues strange and new,
They yield a harvest all their own !

The words of life, cast in the ground,
Spring up in ways to us unknown,
For here the soil is fruitful found,
As in the case of Nature shown.

The slumb'ring forces hasten on,
   The modest blade doth first appear,
Then shoots the stalk, erect, alone,
   And lastly comes the full-grown ear!

And, now, the Angel-reapers, bright,
   Thrust in the sickle, sharp and stroug;
And, gath'ring in the sons of light,
   They save them from the wicked throng.

A magic field of truth and life—
   A wondrous harvest-day is this,
Absolvi ng from earth's war and strife,
   And bearing us to endless bliss!

There, in the heav'nly garner stored,
   What songs of triumph shall we sing?
And to our Lord—the loved, adored—
   What grateful tribute shall we bring?

We'll bring our hearts to Him, the slain,
   Adored by brilliant hosts above!
We'll sing our songs, in grateful strain,
   Responsive to his boundless love!

THE SOWER AND THE SEED.

Jesus—Sower of the seed——
   Source of ev'ry gift divine,
Sow in us Thy word indeed,
   And in mercy on it shine,
That it may spring up apace,
   Firm and deeply rooted be;
Nurtured still in truth and grace,
   May we thus be found in Thee!

Jesus—Sower of the seed—
Source of all that's good and true,
Greatly we Thy blessing need
While our calling we pursue ;
Jesus, we Thy promise claim,
Promise made in times of yore,
When assembled in Thy name,
" Lo, I'm with you evermore !"

Jesus—Sower of the seed—
Source exclusive of success,
Graciously Thy kingdom speed,
All our efforts kindly bless !
Called are we Thy light to bear,
Further still Thy truth to sound,
Until ALL Thy word shall hear,
E'en to Earth's remotest bound !

Jesus—Sower of the seed—
Source of sweetest bliss to me,
When distrest—in greatest need,
All my joy I find in Thee ;
Jesus—be my refuge here,
Fold me in Thine arms of love ;
Be my shield when danger's near,
Be my crown in realms above !

THE MORNING COMETH, AND ALSO THE NIGHT.

ISA. 21: 12.

The promised day is dawning
In glory from on high—
Yet, ere the blessed morning,
Night deepens o'er the sky !

Upon Earth's erring children
　The curse will have its way ;
Nor, till its strength be wasted,
　Will beauty crown the day !

The soft'ning light declineth,
　The ev'ning shades are nigh ;
The sun no longer shineth,
　The stars appear on high !

My weary limbs are ailing,
　My heart is sad and sore ;
For ALL things now are failing,
　Save He, whom I adore !

O, blessed truth ! This knowing,
　My faith is firm and strong ;
And peace, still onward flowing,
　Cheers me Life's path along !

The night—tho' much bewailing,
　The dawning doth appear ;
The darkness now is paling,
　The sky will soon be clear !

O blessed Hope—how cheering !
　All sorrow flies away ;
And night, now disappearing,
　Will change to endless day !

Sweet morn of joyous waking,
　From ev'ry burden free ;
The promised day is breaking
　In bliss, O Lord, in Thee !

Then, still in God confiding,
　My faith be firm and true ;

Thy promised time abiding,
And vict'ry still pursue !

The morning surely cometh,
The night must pass away,
And he that, faithful, runneth,
Shall gain the happy day!

O, day of Hope's fruition,
Of heav'nly peace and joy,
When acts of grateful worship
Shall heart and tongue employ!

While shadows still do linger
Around me in the way ;
Be Thou, O blest Redeemer,
To me the light of day !

The night, tho' dark and dreary,
If Thou be with me there,
May find me sad and weary,
Yet free from grim despair !

Thou art, O blessed Jesus,
The light of life to me ;
And, in the dark uneasy,
I seek my rest in Thee !

"BEHOLD, I COME QUICKLY."

Behold, I come quickly,
Ye boasters and proud ;
The heavens in darkness,
The earth will I shroud.

To God in deep anguish,
  In fear you may cry;
But in that dread moment,
  No aid shall be nigh !

Behold, I come quickly,
  In judgment arrayed;
Nor sentence shall linger,
  Nor wrath shall be stayed.
The proud and the scoffing,
  Tho' long they have stood,
Shall witness with terror
  The frowns of their God !

Behold, I come quickly,
  Full long have I borne
Your sins and your follies,
  Your taunt and your scorn !
My patience is wasted—
  The mercy it sheds,
Now vengeance, deserved,
  Descends on your heads !

Behold, I come quickly,
  Ye sinners shall mourn,
And wish you had perished
  When erst you were born.
The doom of the wicked,
  What tongue can express ?
Your woe and your torment,
  Your pain and distress ?

Behold, I come quickly,
  Ye loved ones of God ;
Your tears I have witnessed,
  Your cries have I heard.

Though men may despise you,
Their wrath disregard ;
Your end shall be glorious,
And great your reward !

Behold, I come quickly,
Ye saints shall rejoice,
And praise Me your Saviour
With heart and with voice.
Your hopes now are certain,
You cannot mistake ;
The souls I have purchased,
I will not forsake !

Behold, I come quickly,
The time is at hand ;
Your patience much longer
I will not demand.
In life ye have owned me,
Your Master and Lord ;
In death my sweet presence
Shall be your reward !

Behold, I come quiekly,
O, be not dismayed ;
The day of salvation
Shall not be delayed !
On angels' swift pinions
Your souls shall be borne
To heaven's high mansions,
To glory's bright throne !

LINES ON DEATH.

O, Death—what dismal tho'ts to every heart,
What gloomy fear it brings, and what dismay !

The very name, so dread, disturbs our souls
And makes us, trembling, wish 'twere far away.
'Tis, thus, we banish every thought of death
To set our hearts at ease; yet death is nigh,
E'en at the door, and seeks admittance there,
With high commission armed, intent to bear us
All away. Its mandates—ever active—
Alike both strong and feeble must obey;
No age exempt, nor sex, nor any state—
Nor from its ruthless hand can wealth protect;
Nor virtues pure, nor aught that men esteem,
Can shield us from the inveterate foe!

When morn's sweet light doth gently on us dawn,
Or mid-day sun in fullest splendor shines,
Or evening breezes softly o'er us sweep,
Or 'round us midnight shades in silence hang;
When, wrapt in thought, we gaze on Nature's works,
Or sleep, unconscious of the world around,
Whate'er we do, or in whatever state we be,
There death stands ready-harnessed for his work,
And, both by day and midnight's lonely hours,
Doth boldly seize the objects of pursuit!

Thus. what the dismal night-shades left untouched,
Unwarned at morning falls beneath his pow'r;
In broad daylight the work is still pursued,
And stout hearts break, and tears incessant flow.
Till ev'ning hides the melancholy scene,
And screens from mortal sight the horrid work.
With lion-strength he grasps earth's hapless ones
And bears them from the field without delay.
Unnumbered myriads each day are borne
From life's arena; and myriads more,
Unknown, succeed and follow in their wake!

The man of years—the aged and in firm—
Already feels death's heavy hand imposed,
And soon must leave his kindred here below :
The man of middle age he likewise takes away ;
Sweet children at his bidding fall ; and e'en
The tender babe, whose infant spirit scarce
Began to be, is crushed beneath his sway.
He cares for none, nor spares—both rich and poor,
Both high and low, are all to him the same :
He favors none, but treats them all alike !

Such is the Tyrant's power, and such his sway,
That none may hope indulgence or escape ;
His ceaseless wrath—of blood insatiate—
High justice owns—the bitter fruit of sin,
And Death is absolute in all his ways—
Of other monarchs none so much to dread ;
To him must all submit, both small and great,
When once the fatal day—Death's day—appears.
That solemn day is near—on every hand
We see such signs as wise men ought to heed.
Each day he bears some loved one swift away,
And God thus loudly speaks : Come, mortals, seek
In peace to meet the stern decree of death !

REFLECTIONS ON THE RESURRECTION.

Though death despoil this mortal frame,
And quench awhile the vital flame ;
I know from death this frame shall rise,
And live beyond the vaulted skies !

The seed that's cast into the ground,
Though now in vile corruption found,

Shall truly thence spring up again,
And deck with green the life-clad plain !

So shall this frame, despoiled by death,
Once feel Christ's all-reviving breath—
Awake from this its couch of clay,
And reign, restored, in endless day !

The rescued one, in glory found,
With peerless beauty there is crowned ;
And who, with human skill, can paint
The rapture of the risen saint !

HEAVEN: OR, THE EVERLASTING REST.

There is a Home than all moré sweet,
With life divine—with bliss replete ;
A Home for which my spirit longs,
Secure, enriched with sacred songs ;
Where Faith and Love most swectly blend,
Where friend communion holds with friend !

'Tis found where saints in rapture meet,
Where spirits pure such spirits greet ;
Where robed in splendor Jesus reigns,
And angels chant their lofty strains,
Where God, enthroned, exalted sits—
And, grateful, each to Him submits !

'Tis found where all is love and peace,
Where triumphs full redeeming grace ;
Where saints, adoring, lowly bend,
And songs of praise to Christ ascend ;
Where shining hosts before Him fall
And crown JEHOVAH—Lord of ALL !

www.ingramcontent.com/pod-product-compliance
Lightning Source LLC
Chambersburg PA
CBHW030550040726
47497CB00008B/2655